# Weaving Fire

**M.V. Venkatram** (1920–2000) is a Sahitya Akademi award-winning Tamil author. He was born in Kumbakonam in Thanjavur district, Tamil Nadu. A prolific writer, Venkatram has authored over two hundred literary works, including novels, novellas, short plays, poetry and essays, which were published in illustrious newspapers and literary magazines.

In 1948, he established *Thenee*, a literary magazine. Prominent Tamil writers contributed to this publication. He was also the honorary editor for the Tamil literary magazine *Paalam*, where his novel *Ears* was serialized. In addition to writing, he also undertook many translations from English and Hindi. He translated biographies of Raja Ram Mohan Roy, Mahatma Gandhi, Jawaharlal Nehru, Bhagat Singh and Indira Gandhi.

**Sumi Kailasapathy** migrated from Sri Lanka to the USA in the early 1990s. She received her bachelor's degree in Economic and Political Science from Wellesley College, Massachusetts and her graduate degrees in Political Science from the New School for Social Research, New York. She lives with her family in Ann Arbor, Michigan and enjoys reading, playing the veena and working on political campaigns.

# Weaving Fire

## M.V. Venkatram

Translated from the Tamil original by
### Sumi Kailasapathy

Published by
Rupa Publications India Pvt. Ltd 2022
7/16, Ansari Road, Daryaganj
New Delhi 110002

*Sales Centres:*
Allahabad Bengaluru Chennai
Hyderabad Jaipur Kathmandu
Kolkata Mumbai

Copyright © The literary estate of M.V. Venkatram 2022
Translation copyright © Sumi Kailasapathy
Introduction copyright © Swarnavel Eswaran Pillai and Ramaswami Mahalingam

Published by arrangement with Kalachuvadu Publications.

This is a work of fiction. Names, characters, places and incidents are either the product of the author's imagination or are used fictitiously and any resemblance to any actual person, living or dead, events or locales is entirely coincidental. The contents of this book reflect the views of the author and translator. The Tamilnadu Textbook and Educational Services Corporation is not responsible for the same.

All rights reserved.
No part of this publication may be reproduced, transmitted, or stored in a retrieval system, in any form or by any means, electronic, mechanical, photocopying, recording or otherwise, without the prior permission of the publisher.

P-ISBN: 978-93-5520-887-3
E-ISBN: 978-93-5520-897-2

First impression 2022

10 9 8 7 6 5 4 3 2 1

The moral right of the author has been asserted.

Printed in India

This book is sold subject to the condition that it shall not, by way of trade or otherwise, be lent, resold, hired out, or otherwise circulated, without the publisher's prior consent, in any form of binding or cover other than that in which it is published.

# MISSION STATEMENT

This is an initiative of the Tamil Nadu Textbook and Educational Services Corporation (TNTB & ESC) under the aegis of one of the announcements for the year 2021–22 by the Honourable Minister for School Education Thiru. Anbil Mahesh Poyyamozhi to identify and translate into English, Tamil literary works, that they might enhance the reach of Tamil antiquity, tradition and contemporaneity and enrich world literature, and to also translate significant literary voices from other Dravidian languages into Tamil. Both ventures are to be undertaken as either independent or joint publications with collaborating publishers.

**Members, Academic Advising Committee (Translation)**
1. Dr R. Balakrishnan, IAS, Researcher and Writer
2. Thiru. S. Ramakrishnan, Writer
3. Thiru. S. Madasamy, Educationist

**Project Execution Team**
1. Thiru. Dindigul I. Leoni, Chairperson, TNTB & ESC
2. Tmt. R. Gajalakshmi, IAS, Managing Director, TNTB & ESC
3. Dr S. Kannappan, Member Secretary, TNTB & ESC
4. Thiru. R. Dhayalan, Financial Advisor, TNTB & ESC
5. Dr T. S. Saravanan, Joint Director (Translations), TNTB & ESC
6. Thiru. P. A. Arumugam, Deputy Director (Publications), TNTB & ESC
7. Dr P. Saravanan, Assistant Director (Publications), TNTB & ESC
8. Thiru. M. Appanasamy, Consultant, TNTB & ESC
9. Tmt. Mini Krishnan, Co-ordinating Editor, TNTB & ESC

# Translator's Note

Kannan, Kausalai and Hema will stay with you long after you have finished reading this book. The significance of *Weaving Fire* lies not only in its realistic portrayal of the three main characters as they struggle through poverty, famine, floods, debt and many other challenges but also in its depiction of these characters as full-fledged humans who are funny, generous, loyal, sexually adventurous and so on. While these characters live within the strict social norms of the Saurashtrian community of Tamil Nadu, they also continuously transgress the norms that limit and oppress them.

This novel does not revolve around heroes and villains like in typical working-class stories. The characters are riddled with contradictions and emotional conflicts like most ordinary people. Their continuous emotional struggle to survive, on the one hand, and to find meaning and pleasure in their harsh lives, on the other, leads to plenty of heartaches and tragedy. At the end of the book, one can empathize with many of these characters not because they are flawless or heroic but because one understands their choices and actions through the development of the storyline and characters. M.V. Venkataram has definitely left an impressive mark on Tamil literature through this novel. I am honoured to translate this noteworthy novel so that readers in the Anglophone world might also enjoy it.

Translating a novel in the era of the Internet influences one's word choices. To allow readers to obtain additional information and context for this novel, I have used spellings and words whose meanings are easily accessible online. So, if someone would ask me why I have used the word *jari* instead of *jarikai* as it is usually pronounced in Tamil, it is because one can easily find the word 'jari' on the Internet.

Chapter three of this novel is a demographic, social and cultural description of the Saurashtrian community. The author inserted this after the first two chapters. In the beginning, I was not sure whether it should be moved to the appendix or not. But later, I decided to leave it as is, as I did not want to second guess the author's intentions. I also did not change any of the demographic facts reported by the author in that chapter, as it is a moving target. Therefore, it is important to remember that the facts stated in that chapter are frozen in time from when the book was first published in 1975.

I owe much to Mini Krishnan for encouraging me to take on the task of translating this book. Since this is my first attempt at translating a novel into English, Mini guided me at every step of the process. She helped me remap and recast my translation, developing it in such a way that non-Tamil readers could feel the mood and the flavour of the original language. She did the first round of editing on this book with great patience and care. N. Asokan's fluency in Tamil and English helped with the final round of editing and made sure that every word had the right meaning. I owe him a lot. Similarly, Ram Mahalingam, who hails from the same region as the author, helped me understand many cultural, social and political nuances of the language in the book. Thank you for all your insights, Ram.

I would like to thank the Rupa team—Sneha Bhagwat for her meticulous editing, and Dibakar Ghosh for taking on this publication. I am also grateful to the Tamil Nadu Textbook Corporation (TNTB) for selecting this book to be translated and published.

Sumi Kailasapathy
2022

# Introduction
## M.V. Venkatram: Weaving the Slices of Life

M.V. Venkatram (1920–2000) or MVV, as he is popularly known, is a Tamil writer mostly known for his work during the latter half of the twentieth century. MVV is synonymous with Kumbakonam, since he never left the famous town near Thanjavur—he lived and died there. More importantly, the spaces in and around Kumbakonam serve as a backdrop for most of his stories. His life, like some of his novels, was also an epic. He was born into a wealthy family of weavers who had migrated from Saurashtra in Gujarat and settled in Tamil Nadu long ago. His rich background allowed him to acquire an English-medium education. He inherited and engaged in the flourishing family business from a young age. However, what set him apart from the rest of the family was his investment in literature. He wrote his first short story 'Chittu Kuruvi' (House Sparrow) at the age of sixteen and got it published in *Manikkodi*, a prestigious literary journal committed to providing an avenue for serious modern Tamil writers. Soon after, he wrote sixteen short stories and built a reputation as a notable Tamil writer, even though he graduated in economics from a local college. Thanjai Prakash, the eminent writer and critic from Thanjavur, has noted that MVV's unique literary value lies in his original outlook as a free thinker who privileged inclusivity in his writings.

MVV's primary business was manufacturing highly expensive silk borders for saris. There was a time when he was surrounded by wealth and known for his indulgence, particularly with his friends. His unwavering faith in his friends led to him being cheated in business, resulting in a downturn in his fortune when his children were young and needed security. As a middle-aged man, he had to give up his literary style of writing. Despite working for twelve hours a day as a writer for pulp magazines, he found it challenging to make ends meet. MVV scholar Prof. V. Kalyanaraman and biographer Ravisubramaniyan co-edited a volume of the author's collected short stories on his birth centenary, titled *M.V. Venkatram Sirukathaigal*. The volume detailed the aesthetic value of MVV's literature, even as he catered to popular magazines' general readership.

MVV's work has two notable thematic preoccupations. First, his investment in mythology—particularly invoking women figures entrenched in the Indian/Tamil psyche, like Akalya/Akalikai from the Ramayana or Tilottama from the Mahabharata—to address contemporary issues like gender inequity through the ornate narrative universe of the epics. Unlike other pre-eminent Tamil writers, like Pudhumaipithan, MVV's writing focusses on catharsis and reaffirming the status quo by upholding societal (patriarchal) values. However, he exalts the women in his stories for their patience and suffering.

The second notable thematic preoccupation in his writing is detailing the social issues of his time through the lens of realism. *Weaving Fire* could be read in this light. The novel focusses on two significant issues. At the sociological level, it documents the mundane struggles and lives of the Saurashtrians, a diasporic community, maintaining their unique cultural identity despite it being mostly integrated into the local Tamil culture. Through *Weaving Fire*, MVV critiques the Saurashtrian community's commitment to outdated traditions, like being overly hospitable to the bridegroom for six months after marriage, which are a source of financial and psychological stress to the working-class weaving community.

The novel also offers detailed descriptions of the disruptions of life and livelihood of the weavers during the monsoon. Without deeply engaging with the struggles of the weavers who were at the mercy and goodwill of the wholesale merchants, it only makes a cursory reference to the Communist Party actively fighting for fair wages. The novel portrays the weavers' struggles and sufferings through the voices of weavers affiliated with various political parties. While discussing the weavers' political affiliations, MVV mentions only two parties (Congress and the Communists). In contrast, the Dravidian parties are referred using their sarcastic colloquial abbreviations (like 'Thina Kanna', the expanded colloquial form of the first two letters, instead of 'Thi Ka' to refer to Dravidar Kazhagam).

When the novel came out, Congress was the ruling party and K. Kamaraj, also called Kamarajar, was the chief minister. E.V. Ramasamy, also known as Periyar, was the leader of Dravidar Kazhagam (DK) during this time. Periyar supported Kamarajar and hailed his rule as 'Pachai Tamilan' (authentic Tamilian), referring to Kamarajar, the first non-Brahmin chief minister of Tamil Nadu post-Independence, who hailed from a backward caste. MVV sarcastically points out Kamarajar's government's inability to help the poor. In the novel, one of the weavers makes fun of the Pachai Tamilan's rule for its inability to supply adequate provisions through the price-regulated public distribution system. Despite MVV's association with the Congress Party (he unsuccessfully ran for the position of a ward counselor as a Congress candidate), his politics was dented by his ambiguous and critical stance against the Dravidian movement, which comes through in some of his works.

At the psychological level, the novel explores the love triangle between Kannan, the protagonist of the novel, and the two women who are in love with him. Kausalai, Kannan's wife, loves her husband and supports him in his journey to become a successful businessman. Her dedication to her husband is, however, thwarted by her friend, Hema, a widow from the community. Despite MVV's ambivalence toward Periyar, paradoxically, Hema comes across as a widow who is willful and agentic. She follows through on her desires, embodying Periyar's conception of an empowered woman who is not fettered by the socially imposed restrictions on widows. When Hema tries to help with Kannan's struggles, she comes across as a rational problem-solver with a long-term perspective. Hema is a forerunner to other self-possessed agentic widows in Tamil literature, such as Indu in *Amma Vandhaal*.

*Weaving Fire* attempts to balance the tensions between external social changes with the internal desires and passions of a Saurashtrian weaver while vividly portraying his life in Kumbakonam.

Swarnavel Eswaran
Ramaswami Mahalingam
2022

## Chapter 1

There was neither lightning nor thunder. It was as if the rain had made a pact with the earth to demolish anything deemed unnecessary. The rain was coming down steady and heavy. It had been raining for two days. Now, it seemed that it might finally cease by afternoon, by which time the sun was scorching. By the evening, the clouds were roaming around like soldiers. Then, as if it had been waiting for everyone to fall asleep, the rain bore down again with a new vengeance. The mayhem unleashed by the skies over the past two days had left the people and the land exhausted.

As the rain finally died down in the afternoon and nightfall approached, they rejoiced saying, 'It will not rain anymore, we have survived.' In that confidence, they slept peacefully. Then, suddenly, when the rain started assaulting them again, they were stunned.

One of the elements of nature was teasing them; the people

could not take that anymore, and the fearful earth wept.

Kausalai woke up first. The roof had sprung a leak, which gradually drenched the mat that she was sleeping on. It seeped through her blouse, touched her breasts and woke her up. She opened her eyes at the refreshingly cool sensation. Half-asleep, in the pitch darkness, she could not see anything.

Darkness concealed everything like maya, yet the furore of the rain was palpable. She sensed that the rain had entered the house. Fear engulfed her. She reached out to Kannan, her husband, lying beside her. He was dead to the world. She instantly realized that the rain had invaded their home like an uninvited guest and was ravaging everything.

'Please wake up, it's raining hard,' she muttered, trying to wake her husband up.

Kannan, oblivious even to the fast-invading sogginess, woke up and clasped Kausalai's hands.

'Water is entering the house; how can you sleep, unaware of the dampness?' she yanked herself away from him and jumped up.

'Turn on the lights!' Kannan called out as he got up. Only then did he notice the darkness and damp that had enveloped them. 'How did the water get in here? Is it leaking? Don't we need to check on the looms? Kausalai, quickly turn on the light!'

She was not waiting for his orders. Wading through the darkness, she exclaimed, 'No lights!'

'How can there be electricity in this rain?' replied Kannan, now wide awake. Instead of the usual dull patter of the rain, he heard it gushing down. He could feel the rivulets of water streaming about his feet. Worry overcame him when he thought of the plight of his looms.

'This cursed rain will stop only after destroying our town! Kausalai, have you picked up the baby?'

'Yes, I've picked her up; good thing Raji is not wet.'

Feeling his way through the darkness, he opened the almirah and took out the matchbox and night lamp. With the help of that tiny light, he found the flashlight and inspected the leaking roof. The two glass[1] roof tiles had dislodged. Rainwater was entering the house freely through this gaping hole, bathing the two looms and their platforms. Kannan was stunned for a second. He snapped out of it when he heard Kausalai shouting, 'Aiyyo amma!' Worried that something had happened to their baby, he rushed toward his wife.

'Kausalai, Raji?'

'Nothing has happened to Raji; water is pouring down the looms—we're going to be ruined!'

'Did you yell because of that? Is Raji asleep or awake?'

'She's wide awake,' she said, pointing to the baby snuggling against her breasts. She was nursing the baby while standing there.

'Okay, leave the baby in the hammock and come here. The hammock didn't get wet, did it?'

---

[1] In some houses, two glass panes are substituted for the usual clay tiles in the roof to allow sunlight to enter the house. These panes usually do not fit perfectly with the clay tiles and are dislodged easily.

'No.'

'Leave the baby and come here. Let's roll up both the looms and put them away.'

Kausalai laid the baby back in the hammock. Since she had abruptly stopped nursing Raji, the baby started kicking and screaming. Ignoring the baby, she raced to help her husband.

Wielding the flashlight, they both approached the loom. Theirs was a tile-roofed house. But the torrential rains had soaked the tiles and the water had begun to seep through.

Like a thief searching for the most valuable items, the water was heading toward the silk spools and the jari[2] on the looms, staining them. These two silk looms were Kannan's livelihood; he owned both of them, of which he was immensely proud. He had endured great hardships to acquire them. He was now dreaming of expanding from two looms to three and even five.

This damn rain was dissolving those dreams!

One of the looms had an entirely gold weave, which was of great value. So, they began rolling that up first. The baby in the hammock was screaming; her lament mirrored her parents' distress.

'I can't believe I slept through all this!' Kannan moaned.

'When you work so hard during the day, why wouldn't you sleep through all this? Who would've guessed that the rain would cause so much devastation?' Kausalai replied.

---

[2] Gold thread

'The rain has pulled a Chinaman[3] on us. If it suddenly jumps and devours us, what can we do? Look at this! The cloth is soaking wet. The jari is shedding and forming fuzz balls. If we roll it up and leave it, what will happen to it by tomorrow?'

This was not the time to worry about tomorrow. With Kausalai's help, he quickly rolled up the silk and the jari warps. Then, he rolled up the second loom. He covered both the looms with a canvas and placed them on a plank near the baby's hammock for safekeeping.

'At least this survived. If we had slept a little longer, even the loom platform would have dissolved away in the rain, it looks like...' Kannan trailed off.

When Kausalai lifted the baby and started nursing her, Raji stopped crying. 'If we fix the glass roof tiles, it'll stop the leak,' Kausalai said.

'How do I fix it now? If I get up there to fix it, the tiles will be pulverized, and I'll fall down with the roof,' Kannan responded.

'Am I asking you to climb on the roof? If you can just adjust the dislodged glass panes with a pole—'

'I can't adjust the tiles now. If the tiles slip and fall, we will have to leave this house at once.'

Kausalai could not come up with any other solutions to escape from the wetness. She felt sad and exhausted all of a

---

[3] Here, the author is comparing the rain with the 1967 Indo–China War, where the People's Liberation Army had launched surprise attacks against Indian posts.

sudden. The baby found solace in the embrace of the mother. Oblivious to the danger facing her parents, she was cooing in a melodic raga. Kannan was trying his best to divert the water flow and keep the dry areas from the aggressive rain. But, it was a losing battle as the leaking water widened its reach. The rain intensified and the water continued to spread throughout the house.

'It's going to be Shivaratri[4] tonight. Why are you getting wet? Come and sit here,' Kausalai called out. The baby had fallen asleep while Kausalai nursed her. She laid the baby back in the hammock.

The rain continued to drone on outside. 'I will stop only after destroying you,' it seemed to challenge Kannan. He, too, was acting as though he had accepted the challenge and was moving things around, attempting to save them from getting wet.

How long can one do sundry chores when one wakes up in the middle of the night? He was tired. *Let whatever is to happen, happen*, he thought courageously. He took off his wet clothes and changed into another *veshti*[5].

Kausalai's shadow loomed larger than life in the lamplight, making her look very attractive.

Kannan walked towards her to the bed and said, 'I haven't seen rain like this in my lifetime!'

---

[4]Shivaratri is a Hindu festival celebrated annually where ardent devotees of Lord Shiva stay awake all night.
[5]Veshti is a white cloth wrap for the lower body that men wear in Tamil Nadu.

'It's raining as if the devil itself was here!' she said.

'Raji is sleeping soundly!'

'When her tummy is full, what other concerns does she have?'

'Let her sleep well,' Kannan said with a sigh. With that sigh, he forgot about the rain and the destruction it was inflicting upon them. To beat the cold, he needed some warmth.

Kausalai welcomed him. The rope bed heaved.

## Chapter 2

The sky was clear by dawn. The sun was scorching the earth like an enraged tyrant emerging after a rebellion. 'Are you still asleep, Kannan? The town is drowning and you're sleeping like a baby?' a booming voice woke Kannan up.

He sat up, stretching; his whole body was aching as he hazily remembered the events of the previous night.

'You live in a tile-roofed house; you can sleep peacefully. Our story is different!' said Jembu Rangasamy.

'Varuna[6] doesn't show mercy just because you live in a tile-roofed house. I have rolled up both the partially woven pieces of cloth. Kausalai, have you put the yarns out to dry?' Kannan asked.

'I have,' she responded from the kitchen.

---

[6]The Hindu god of water

'What is your news?' inquired Kannan of Rangan.

'What's my news? My news, eh? Hyder-period[7] mud wall collapsed. Only a *saan*[8] between me and death. If I had rolled over in my sleep, the wall would have crashed on my head. I survived due to God's grace! I survived despite my parents' bad deeds.'

'You didn't survive despite your parents' bad deeds; you survived because you have to repay the loans you took from your *muthalali*[9],' replied Kannan.

'You own your looms. Why *wouldn't* you say these things?' said Rangan. Five or six years older than Kannan, he had failed to acquire his own looms or a house and was jealous of Kannan and very frustrated because someone younger had been able to achieve what he had not.

Kannan understood his disposition well. 'I've been ruined trying to own looms. It seems like this rain is going to make me a coolie[10] weaver. If the yarn and the jari get wet and are ruined, isn't it a loss for the owner? If the pan is hot, you can let go of it. I am not in such a situation!' Kannan said, visibly annoyed.

---

[7]This refers to a Hyder Ali-period wall, which means very old. The author is referring to Hyder Ali, an eighteenth century Muslim military commander of a portion of the princely state of Mysuru.

[8]A measure of an outspread palm, between the thumb and little finger, approximately six inches

[9]This usually means proprietor or owner of a business. In the weaving industry, which is the case here, it refers to an owner who contracts others to work on his looms.

[10]Hired labour

'All night, I couldn't get a wink of sleep. All four of my children were playing in the rainwater as if they were having fun at the pond. "Don't play with the water!" I said. My second one is very mischievous, right? "Shall I dance in the street, Appa[11]?" he asked. What could I say? As soon as I woke up in the morning, I swept and cleaned the house, and then went to a food stall. You know Govindan's story, don't you?'

'I woke up only after you came here. How am I supposed to know Govindan's story and Gopalan's story?'

'By starving himself, he saved enough money and bought a cow, right? Last night, his cowshed collapsed.'

'Oh! What a pity! What happened to the cow?'

'The shed collapsed on the cow, and it fell, all four legs splayed and gasping for breath. By God's grace, Govindan happened to glance in the direction of the shed. Seeing nothing there, he and his wife rushed out and raised the shed with great difficulty to rescue the cow.'

'Good thing the cow survived!'

'What's the point? It can't even stand and did not nurse her calf in the morning. They couldn't milk it either. He brought the vet, who said that it could take two to three months for the cow to get better.'

'I had already told Govindan, "Don't invest your savings in a cow. You can't afford to feed it; cows have all the problems we humans have. If you invest in a loom, you don't have to

---

[11]Father

feed it; our investment will remain with us." Now he has all the expenses of the cow, and he's out of breath with all that additional work!' said Kannan.

'Well, did your loom survive? Weren't you just saying that it was damaged in this rain as well?'

'Instead of wasting your time chatting, why not stretch out the wet warps that I put out to dry and see what happened to them,' Kausalai interjected.

'I wanted to wait until Saranathan got here,' said Kannan.

'When is he going to come? That politician will be going from one house to another inquiring what happened to each of them. If you are expecting him to come now, nothing is going to get done this morning. Why don't you get going with him,' she said, pointing to Rangasamy.

'Did I say I wouldn't? Muthalali here is the one who hasn't got over his stupor!' quipped Rangan.

'I don't quite own those two looms, yet you have already made me a muthalali!' said Kannan as he stood up.

He and Rangan stretched out one of the warps and inspected it. There was a lot of jari in it. Since the roof tile had fallen on it, more than half of the jari yarns had broken off from the weave and were hanging loose. In the other loom, the silk had been damaged. Kannan was mentally calculating how much time and money were going to be wasted in fixing the two damaged weaves. His stomach lurched. It would take him four to five days of work—a quarter rupee of loss for every rupee of work he had put in.

Rangan felt smug. 'Even your investment looks like it's at risk,' he said feigning sadness.

Kannan understood Rangan's jealousy well, and therefore did not want to admit his weakness before Rangan.

'There has been no loss to the capital. I've been protecting my investment very diligently,' said Kannan, pointing to his body. He was a member of the Hanuman Exercise Club and had a well-toned, muscular body. Rangan suffered from chronic attacks of asthma. If he worked for a day, he had to rest for two. Kannan's response silenced him.

'If the rain stops with this bout, it is going to get very hot. I wonder if it is going to rain again!' said Rangan, trying to change the topic.

'This town cannot withstand another bout of rain.'

'Is Kausalai home?' inquired a female voice, diverting the attention of both the men. As soon as her eyes locked with Kannan's, Hema felt shy and lowered her head. Adjusting her sari, she rushed towards the kitchen.

'All said and done, you are a lucky fellow!' muttered Rangan, lowering his voice.

'What luck has come my way?'

'It's already here,' said Rangan looking towards the kitchen.

'You are cross-eyed, everything looks crooked to you. If Hema has come to see Kausalai, how is that *my* luck?'

'I know who she is here to see. She comes from a well-to-do family. You better be careful with her!'

'Your pettiness truly knows no bounds. What's there between me and her?'

'Aiyyo! I am sorry!' teased Rangan.

Kausalai came out of the kitchen. 'Hema wants to say something to you. She is asking for you,' she informed and returned to the kitchen.

'Go, go! It must be something very important. Go, find out!' mocked Rangan, with a parting laugh.

Kannan felt embarrassed. He descended the steps and stood at the entrance until Rangan disappeared from his view. *What does she have to tell me?* he pondered as he entered the kitchen.

## Chapter 3

Kumbakonam is sandwiched between the rivers Kaveri to the north and the Arasalar to the south. It is famous for its temples as well as its *thirthas*[12]. It is also well known for its cottage industry—silk weaving. Saurashtrians live along the Arasalar and most of them are silk weavers.

Saurashtrians had not always lived in Tamil Nadu. As the name indicates, their origin lies in the Saurashtra kingdom. Mahmud of Ghazni invaded India, and in his attempt to destroy the Hindu religion, he demolished temples and religious idols. During that period, many Saurashtrian families left their homes and moved south to preserve their religion, culture and livelihood. Despite being Brahmins, Saurashtrians are expert

---

[12]In Hinduism, some rivers are considered sacred. Thirthas are pilgrimages that devotees embark on to bathe in these sacred rivers to cleanse their impurities.

weavers. They are renowned for weaving intricate cotton and silk fabrics. Thus, they are not refugees in the traditional sense, since they did not seek help from others. Wherever they relocated, they continued their weaving tradition and made a living.

The kings of Vijayanagara, Mysuru, Madurai and Thanjavur heard about them and welcomed them. They allowed the Saurashtrians to live and work in their kingdoms. They were charged with the responsibility of producing cloth for the royal wardrobes.

They did not think of returning to Saurashtra. Perhaps, South India gave them peace. Although they lived in many regions, like Andhra Pradesh and Karnataka, they eventually settled in Tamil Nadu. Since they have lived in many parts of South India, their language is sprinkled with words from Southern Indian languages, such as Kannada and Telugu.

The current Saurashtrian population is around three or four hundred thousand. They are spread across Madurai, Thanjavur, Kumbakonam, Ayyampettai, Tiruchirappalli and Kanchipuram. Since they have lived in Tamil Nadu for many centuries, they have completely assimilated into the region and have forgotten the land of their origin. Although they have accepted many of the habits of Tamils, they have not abandoned some of their unique characteristics. They also do not marry into other communities.

Predictably, Tamil Brahmins do not accept Saurashtrians as Brahmins, and many Saurashtrians believe that Tamil Brahmins are not true Brahmins. Saurashtrians also have gotras. Each family claims descent from a particular rishi. They also do not marry within a gotra. People marry only within their own village or the adjacent villages, although recent years have seen a change in the community.

As soon as you enter the streets where Saurashtrians live, you know that you have entered a weavers' locale. When you walk along these streets, you see them starching or cleaning their yarn. Often, you will see women and children seated in their front porches, spinning cotton, silk yarn or jari.

The majority of the Saurashtrians of Kumbakonam are expert silk weavers. Kanchipuram silk is very famous. Many Kanchipuram producers purchase Kumbakonam silk saris and sell them with a Kanchipuram seal.

Some of the Saurashtrians who live in Kanchipuram hail from Kumbakonam. You can identify them from the way they dress and conduct themselves. How many dialects exist in Tamil? There is town, religious and caste slang—one can discern a speaker's town and caste from his slang. Saurashtrian Tamil slang is unique. Saurashtrian spoken language also varies from place to place.

Saurashtrians are very religious. They study the Vedas and Upanishads. Most of them worship modestly. Each house has a dedicated place of worship and a shrine room. The weavers who live in densely populated areas allocate a nook for their prayers. They do not eat before completing their prayers for the day.

After Independence, everyone started discussing political and economic matters, right? The dominance of rationalist thinking has penetrated this community as well. Party differences and policy differences have started shaking the loom platforms. Yet, none of these movements have been able to change their women. Saurashtrian women are great temple-goers and believe in going to tirthas.

The majority of the Saurashtrians are very poor and uneducated. They depend on weaving for their livelihood. After Independence, they began to focus on education. Some Saurashtrians, however, are wealthy. They are involved in the textile manufacturing industry, and, in recent years, have started entering other professions as well.

## Chapter 4

In Kumbakonam, Ramachandrapura Street stands adjacent to the Arasalar River. Even though it is wide, the street is full of potholes. These streets are not meant to provide respite from rain or sun but to teach people vigilance. There is no shortage of such 'model' streets in Kumbakonam.

The house in which Kannan and his family lived was numbered 199 to 203. Kannan owned the front portion of the house, numbered 199. In order to acquire one-fifth of that house, he had to endure many hardships. His parents had been living in Thuvarankurichi, which lies in the southwestern part of Kumbakonam; his ancestors had lived in Darasuram, adjacent to the town.

Kannan was born between two older brothers and three younger sisters. The family struggled to make ends meet. Kannan's two elder brothers were already married; their wives not only took care of the household chores but also helped out with the weaving. Two of his sisters had moved out of town and into their respective husbands' houses. His youngest sister was still at home.

Kannan's father was very keen on educating Kannan. His older sons never even stepped into a school. He really wanted to see his younger son get educated and progress in life. Kannan started his education in a *thinnai* school[13] and eagerly continued through his eighth grade in a town school. When he lived at home and, later, when he would come home for his holidays, he helped out with the weaving. Kannan being at the top of his class was a source of great joy for his father. He dreamt of sending his son to a college across the Kaveri River and educating him to become a scholar.

His elder children wrecked Kannan's father's dreams of educating Kannan. Kannan's brothers really did not understand what Kannan was going to achieve with all his education. They were certainly not jealous of him. His elder brothers believed that Kannan should take advantage of his expertise in weaving. Contrary to their father's wishes, Kannan's brothers forced him to become a weaver.

'If you study beyond eighth grade it is not good for your health. Why don't you begin by sitting next to me on the loom and doing the borders? Later, you can sit in the middle and start weaving!' his second brother ordered Kannan.

---

[13] In the olden days, thinnai schools were conducted by a teacher on his front porch.

Korvai saris have a body colour that is different from that of their border. These saris need to be woven by two people. The person who sits on the side and helps with the threading of the border is called *sigida*. Only after learning to do the borders, one is allowed to sit in the middle and weave the body of the sari.

Thus, Kannan was trained in sigida work. He knew how to design jari borders and was also adept at dyeing. While he was attending school, he trained in all these skills at home. His proficiency in these skills eventually became a barrier to his education. He cried and complained that he wanted to continue studying. But, his siblings did not budge from their position of putting him to work alongside them. They smacked him on the back and made him sit with them on the loom platform to weave. He was just fourteen then. Two years later, his father passed away.

When Kannan's father died, his family had already grown in size. The eldest brother, along with his wife and four children, had already left their home. The second brother's wife and Kannan's mother did not get along with each other at all and fought every day. The issue of their mother's care became a contentious topic. The eldest brother argued that he had a big family, and thus withdrew from the debate. The second brother was confused and troubled by the situation.

By then, Kannan had become a full-fledged weaver. He contemplated establishing his own household with his mother. But, the second brother was reluctant to let him go, as Kannan was earning a lot of money. Due to this tug of war, Kannan was hesitant to leave the family household. His old mother tried to bear the grief of the fights with her daughter-in-law as well as she could. However, she was not articulate enough to win arguments against her second daughter-in-law. She even contemplated surrendering by jumping into the neighbourhood temple pond. This used to be the last refuge of the helpless in Kumbakonam.

Kannan understood his mother's plight and could not bear to witness her being treated like a beggar in her own house. He finally took her with him and left his second brother and family, incurring their wrath. His brother did not give him anything when he left—not even a measuring tape or a rod. He had left with only the clothes on his back. He was fuming that his elder brothers were listening to their wives and humiliating their mother. His anger and urgency turned into determination to provide a good life to his mother.

## Chapter 5

Kannan's brothers lived in Thuvarankurichi. Kannan did not want to be near them, so he moved east. He rented a small place on Thoppu Road, adjacent to the Arasalar River. There was enough room for a loom as well as space to cook. Wasn't that enough? On his friends' recommendations, he rented a loom from Jawahar & Co., situated on New Street. The enterprise gave him some money in advance when they provided him the yarn, which he spent on purchasing cooking utensils. Half-starving to save money, he totally immersed himself in his weaving.

Thus began Kannan's independent life. He was determined not to disgrace himself in the eyes of his siblings. He understood the value of money well—not only to satiate his hunger but also to live well. He was also determined to own a home, even if it was only the size of a postage stamp, before getting married. Since he was literate, he continued to read newspapers and magazines and improve his knowledge.

Earlier, bhajans and street theatre had been the only entertainment for the weavers. Nowadays, these activities were less popular. Instead, evenings were spent discussing politics. After nine o'clock in the night, some silk weavers got together by New Street and discussed varying topics, from world politics to family planning. Newspapers were their primary source of information. Kannan occasionally participated in these nightly meetings. No direct benefits accrued to him as a result of participating in these discussions. Rather, there was a downside to them—when he stayed up late into the night, he also delayed starting work the following morning. But, when he participated in these meetings, the other participants started realizing his knowledge of varied matters. People around him started learning about many things from him and began to respect him. This prominence he enjoyed within his community greatly appealed to his vanity.

He knew all the intricacies of weaving and could, at a glance, gauge even weaves with heavier-than-usual warp threads. Even though all weavers were familiar with these intricacies, he was an expert in the technique. His expertise attracted the attention of some local muthalalis.

Ramasamy Iyer of South Street, a big textile industrialist, owned more than a hundred looms. All his weaves were 'big', smothered with jari. His sales of silk saris extended beyond South India, reaching even Sri Lanka. He had a special talent to snag expert weavers like Kannan. Specialists like Kannan were very rare, so muthalalis competed with each other to snatch such weavers when the opportunity arose. Ramasamy Iyer was kind-hearted, but he was also very good at squeezing the maximum effort out of weavers by encouraging them. He was always ready to help them financially during their weddings and other functions. They were all loans, of course, repayable in small instalments through their weaving. But the weavers were very content with him, as they felt he trusted them to lend them money when they needed it. They were all very happy to work for him.

When somebody told him about Kannan, Ramasamy Iyer immediately sent for him. He listened to Kannan's life story and understood all his difficulties.

'You can leave Jawahar & Co., right?' he asked Kannan.

When Kannan had been summoned, he had known he was going to be offered a loom. Jawahar & Co. was a small establishment, which did not offer him the kind of work that matched his expertise. Besides, their wages were very low. He believed that acquiring a loom from Ramasamy Iyer would be good for him. 'I still owe them fifty rupees. If I return that, I can join you,' Kannan responded to Ramasamy Iyer's question.

'I'll give you fifty rupees. I have a house on Ramachandrapura Street. There are two loom platforms there. You can live there. You only have a mother? You can certainly occupy that house. It'll be very comfortable. It has electricity and a well with good water. I'll give you two contract looms. Can you hire another weaver?' asked Ramasamy Iyer.

Kannan had assumed that he would be given a rental loom—he had expected a big job. Even then, he was really surprised that he was being offered two contract looms simply based on trust, without any inquiries about him. Contract looms meant that he would be provided with silk, jari and wages upfront as an advance on his account. When the sari was completed, he would receive a small additional profit as well. Under this arrangement, the weavers got to keep more of their earnings compared to wage workers. Ramasamy Iyer promised to give Kannan two looms. Kannan was going to weave on one; he had to arrange for someone else to work on the other.

Until now, no one had trusted Kannan, not even for an anna. So, this display of trust by his new muthalali astounded him.

'Whatever you decide is fine with me,' said Kannan, recoiling in a mix of modesty and embarrassment.

'You're not like the other fellows. You're educated. You know what is good and bad. As soon as I saw you, I formed a good impression of you. I'll add a profit of ten rupees per sari for you, alright?'

*He's giving me a place to live. He has loaned me three thousand rupees worth of materials! This is above and beyond the wages! He has agreed to pay me ten rupees extra on a sari!* Kannan thought. All this was a completely new experience for Kannan. 'If you say so, it must be right,' Kannan said with gratitude.

'How many saris do you have to complete?'

'Only one. Six more *mulams*[14] to be woven.'

'As soon as you complete that, come back to me. I'll give you the money. Then, you can settle Jawahar & Co.'s account. Now, do you need any money to complete the weaving?'

'No, I don't, and I will return as soon as I complete that work.'

'Look here, *kanna*[15]. You're very young. I am very happy to hear that you moved out to take care of your mother. Do a good job for me for two years. After you save a bit of money, I'll get you married. I'll have the satisfaction of lighting a lamp[16] for a family.'

At that point, Kannan was melting at the kindness showered on him by his new muthalali, which he had not received even from his brothers. He felt shy to let his new boss know that he was determined to buy a house before getting married.

---

[14] The length from the elbow to the tip of the middle finger
[15] Endearing and diminutive form of the name Kannan, usually used to address children and young people.
[16] It is considered a housewife's duty to light the lamp at dusk. Here, the Iyer is saying he will find a wife for Kannan, who can take care of all the wifely household duties.

## Chapter 6

As his muthalali had described, the Ramachandrapura Street house was a very comfortable place. When he moved into the house, Kannan was nearly twenty years old and had never lived in such a nice place. His portion of the house was adjacent to the street. Five or six families lived in the rest of the building and did not disturb him. His section was boarded off from the rest of the house. He only had to venture beyond his section of the house to fetch water from the well or to access the backyard. There were two weaving platforms in the house, and, resting on them, were two wooden rods to roll up the finished fabric. The house was tile-roofed and had electric lamps. There were two lamps right above each weaving platform to facilitate weaving at night. Apart from the kitchen, there was another large room.

Kannan completed the weaving for his former muthalali and settled his accounts within a week. The former muthalali was sad and sent Kannan off with a scolding. When Kannan received the weaving materials and cash for the two looms from Ramasamy Iyer and entered his new house, he was elated, as if he had been granted a new life. He had also found a person to work on the second loom.

Saranathan was from a village near Kumbakonam. Born into a family of weavers, he belonged to the Thevanga Chettiar caste and had completed the tenth grade. He had maintained the accounts for a few textile shops, but he had detailed knowledge of weaving. He had decided to stop working for others, wanting to weave as an independent contractor. He had recently moved to Kumbakonam and rented a house on New Street.

Ramachandrapura Street and New Street were adjacent to each other. Kannan and Saranathan were acquaintances, and Saranathan agreed to weave for Kannan. Contracting with an accomplished weaver like Saranathan gave Kannan great satisfaction. He handed over the responsibility of keeping accounts pertaining to the looms to Saranathan and paid him separately for that. Both of them were very diligent workers.

No one was happier than Kannan's mother. She had never lived so comfortably before. She also helped with the weaving by spinning the silk yarns and getting the jari ready for weaving. If someone else did this work, Kannan would have had to pay them. So, Kannan paid his mother her due wages. He believed her savings would eventually help him, and his mother would also feel enthusiastic about the work if she had her own money. Besides this income, there was also some leftover silk and jari from the two loom contracts. The more money he made, the more enthusiastic Kannan became; his confidence in the possibility of purchasing a home for himself also grew.

When Kannan settled his accounts with Ramasamy Iyer at the end of the first year, there was a small disagreement between them. The muthalali had promised ten rupees of profit per sari. Kannan had calculated that he would get the ten rupees on the usual six-yard saris, but the muthalali argued that he had agreed on that rate for nine-yard saris only. One loom consisted of six six-yard sari lengths or four nine-yard sari lengths. According to that calculation, Kannan lost twenty rupees per loom. Kannan was very upset but was not in a position to show it. He felt that not clearly negotiating the rates had been his own mistake. When the accounts were settled, the boss still owed him five hundred rupees.

'He was talking about nine-yard saris, while I assumed it was six-yard saris,' said Kannan.

'You trusted your muthalali blindly. I'm not denying the fact that he helped you, but he spoke about six-yard saris at the beginning, and then when he realized how fast you worked, he changed his story to nine-yard saris,' said Saranathan, not believing Ramasamy Iyer's words.

'Just let it go. Wasn't it my fault—not clarifying things at the beginning?'

'Are we going to take him to court? We're merely making a judgement. You should not trust someone so completely. We're good weavers. Won't we be able to get a loom somewhere else?'

'He was the first one to trust me and give me a loom; it would be wrong of me to leave him,' said Kannan.

Saranathan was right. Many big muthalalis wanted to profit off of Kannan's weaving skills. They also promised to provide him good accommodation. But, Kannan did not want to be disloyal to his muthalali.

## Chapter 7

The second year did not turn out well for Kannan. Silk weavers went on a strike, demanding higher wages—a reasonable plea given that the wages were not keeping up with the rising cost of living. Even when an entire family, including the wife and children, wove for their livelihood, they could barely keep hunger at bay. The muthalalis knew the weavers' plight but were not willing to accept their demand. So, the weavers had no other option other than going on strike.

Kannan played an active role in the strike, as Saranathan transformed him into a workers' leader. The others propelled Kannan to the forefront of the struggle because he was literate, could read English and was well informed because of all the newspapers he read. Saranathan was a champion of self-help organizations. He had been involved in many common causes in his own village, which had caused animosity between him and the important people of his village. This had eventually forced him to flee from home. He hated rich people. His definition of a rich person was someone who had too much. He considered anyone who had more money than him to be a rich man. He was very energized by the strike and urged Kannan on, enthusiastically.

Weavers were involved in various forms of resistance, such as work stoppages, hunger strikes, satyagraha, protest marches and public meetings. Unlike industrial workers, weavers did not belong to labour unions, and therefore did not enjoy any of the legal protections that unions provided. Since the weavers were independent contractors, they were not bound to work for a particular muthalali and could quit to work for another, if they desired. Due to the absence of a permanent contractual employer–employee relationship, they did not reap the benefits of the protections guaranteed by labour laws.

How long could the weavers be out of work? They were half-starving even when they were fully employed. What would their plight be when they abandoned what little income they had? How long could they protest while starving? Being well-aware of this reality, their muthalalis prolonged the strike, pretending to negotiate with the leaders of the labourers. Finally, the weavers were in such a desperate situation that they did not care whether they got the wage increase as long as they had enough money for a meal. They started blaming the leaders who had instigated them to strike, and Kannan, too, received his share of the blame.

During the strike, Kannan began to understand his

muthalali's true personality. He was a very religious man and wanted to satisfy Mahavishnu as well as Lord Shiva.[17] He wore the religious markings of both religious groups. He also chanted and prayed to both gods. He never ate before feeding at least one beggar. Even though he had all these good qualities, when it came to wage disputes, he was cruel and cold-hearted.

Kannan knew that the muthalalis were plotting to break the strike by creating discord and division among the weavers. An insignificant muthalali announced that he was going to accept the weavers' demand and increase the wages. Even if only a few weavers returned to work, would the strike not start to falter?

Kannan saw that his muthalali was also part of this plot. If Ramasamy Iyer accepted the demand for higher wages, he would have to incur an additional cost of sixteen thousand rupees a year. He could recover this by marking up the sales price on the saris, which he was unwilling to do.

Just as Kannan was disgruntled with his muthalali, he was also furious with Kannan. When he found out that Kannan was speaking at public meetings and taking part in satyagraha protests, he was infuriated. He had seen Kannan speaking at public meetings like a seasoned politician—calm and collected. He was also one of the negotiators who met with the muthalalis. He put forward the weavers' demands in a clear and moving manner. When his muthalali observed all this, his anger grew.

---

[17]In Hinduism, Vaishnavites worship Lord Vishnu and Shaivites worship Lord Shiva. Kannan's muthalali wanted to play it safe by following the rituals for and worshipping both these deities.

While the weavers were on strike, he summoned Kannan and admonished him that even if he was unwilling to withdraw from the strike, it was wrong for him to be aggressively leading it. His whole life might be ruined because of his actions, the muthalali warned.

'The demand for a higher wage in light of the continuous increase in the cost of living is only fair,' said Kannan politely. He even tried to inveigle the muthalali into becoming a mediator himself, saying 'If muthalali sets his mind to it, you can easily settle this dispute.'

'I didn't call you to debate this. Let our unions reach a decision and we will be bound by it. Why should you be involved in this brawl?'

'I need to follow the path that the town is taking. I have a personal duty as well,' said Kannan, scratching his head.

'When you were begging for food, did your union help you? Who helped you?'

'What does that have to do with this matter?'

'Is there no relationship? Can you forget the people who fed you when you were hungry? You came to me like an orphan. I gave you a house and thousands of rupees worth of weaving supplies—this is a fine way to repay your debt! When you get to eat to your heart's content, gratitude begins to fade,' Ramasamy Iyer admonished, losing his patience. He was expecting to subdue Kannan, but instead, when Kannan began talking back, he found himself starting to raise his voice.

Kannan had not forgotten the help he had received from

Ramasamy Iyer but was very uncomfortable when his muthalali started listing the favours out. Kannan understood that his muthalali had helped him out of his own selfish motives. Gradually, he realized why his muthalali showed so much empathy and consideration towards expert weavers like him. When he gave you fifty or hundred rupees, he was filling his pockets with five hundred and thousand rupees. Initially, Kannan thought that the profits made on investments were fair, as it was the compensation for capital. But, when Ramasamy Iyer was not willing to meet even the basic needs of the weavers, he began to feel a great bitterness. Yet, Kannan was reluctant to hit back with words.

*All said and done, when I was drifting around, he was the one who gave me refuge. I should not make him an enemy,* was the thought that kept Kannan's tongue in check. He left Ramasamy Iyer's office without responding to his muthalali's angry outburst.

Despite the valiant efforts of the labour leaders, the strike began to fizzle out. The weavers began weaving secretly; later they openly disregarded the public statements released by the unions. This forced the union leadership to come to an agreement with the muthalalis, despite gaining only a token wage hike. Ultimately, the strike failed.

Kannan was afraid that he might have to leave Ramasamy Iyer. But, it seemed that his muthalali's anger had subsided with the failure of the strike. This was how Kannan benefited as a result of the failed strike!

## Chapter 8

The handloom market has never been very stable—an upswing for a few years is always followed by a downturn. After the strike, due to the general downturn in the economy, the textile market took a beating, and the silk fabric market, in particular, was very badly affected. The silk fabric trade depended on silk grown in the Mysuru region. A failure of seasonal rains in the region caused silk production to collapse, and as a result, silk prices rose. The manufacturers were not able to sell their fabrics at higher prices to keep pace with the increase in the cost of raw materials. Further, with the purchasing power of the currency dipping and the cost of essential items rapidly rising, consumers could not afford to buy luxury items like silks.

Small muthalalis who owned only a few tens of looms were squeezed badly. They purchased their raw materials, such as silk yarn and jari, on credit. If they could not make their loan payments on time, it ruined their credit rating. Once their credit rating was impaired, lenders thought twice before loaning to them. These small muthalalis tried to sell their products at a modest price to save their credit rating. They truly believed that the next season would be good, and they would compensate for this loss. But, when the next season also turned out to be disastrous, their economic condition collapsed. When the lenders found out that the small muthalalis were selling their products well below market prices, they started pressuring them to repay their loans. Many businesses, like Jawahar & Co., which had lent Kannan his first loom, went broke, paying a quarter or one-eighth of a rupee to settle their loans.

Even the muthalalis that had a hundred or two hundred looms were in a quandary. Since both silk and jari are expensive raw materials, how much could they stockpile items made from them? They, too, curtailed their production and shrank their businesses.

When the muthalalis themselves were being driven away like chaff in the wind, what chance did ordinary weavers stand? Most lost their livelihood. Many wove for half the wages; some, ashamed to beg in the presence of their fellow townsmen, moved far away from their hometowns. Unfortunately, these weavers did not possess other skills—not even begging!

During these years, Kannan's finances deteriorated. His already strained relationship with his muthalali complicated further. Since Kannan was an expert weaver, his muthalali could not let him go. At the same time, due to lack of work, he could not get him to work much either. Kannan understood the confounding situation that the bigger muthalalis in town, including his own, were in. Earlier, if a weaver came to work for his muthalali, they would immediately be provided with the necessary yarn and working capital. But, during this economic downturn, the muthalali delayed this by four or five days and, sometimes, even ten to fifteen days, giving unconvincing excuses. In the meantime, weavers had to roam around in a limbo, without any cash and with empty stomachs.

Can one blame the muthalalis for everything? Newly woven saris crammed not only cupboards but were also stacked up on floor mats as if that had been put to sleep under the covers. Not a single buyer.

Ramasamy Iyer was renowned as someone who was very good at what he did. But even his reputation was being questioned. Silk fabric salesmen were reluctant to lend him raw materials. Since the muthalali did not have sufficient cash to buy them outright, he had to juggle between loans and cash purchases. It was risky to liquidate a fabric business, as not even half the capital could be redeemed. With no other choice, he had to hold his breath and ride on.

By this time, Kannan had matured and did not wish to antagonize his muthalali or seem ungrateful. Even if Kannan left Ramasamy Iyer, he would not be able to find a comfortable place to live. So, he bent over backwards to accommodate his muthalali's demands. Ramasamy Iyer not only decreased Kannan's wages but also the agreed-upon profit margin per sari. Furthermore, he started imposing hefty penalties when he found 'mistakes' in a sari. Kannan bore all this stoically.

However, the situation worsened. The muthalali began to feel ashamed of himself when he could not deliver the weavers with the raw materials and cash, even after giving them lousy excuses to justify the prolonged delays. Gone were the days when he could afford to pay high wages. Now, he was finding it difficult to even pay the weavers what was due to them. He was miserable because the weavers saw through his vulnerability. He 'secretly' pawned his land and jewellery to save his reputation. But, somehow or other, the weavers found out.

Jari is manufactured in Surat, a city that was part of the Bombay region back then. Gujaratis monopolized this business. They generously lend to silk manufacturers, based on trust. The talk among the weavers was that the muthalali was obtaining excessive amounts of jari from them and was pawning them for cash.

Ramasamy Iyer rarely spoke to the weavers anymore, leaving that to his accountant. But, he would occasionally have long conversations with Kannan, not only about work but also other matters. He began confiding in Kannan, placing him in a dilemma: Kannan could not demand what his muthalali owed him, as he knew the muthalali's financial difficulties. The muthalali grew affectionate towards Kannan.

Kannan began to fear that he, too, might have to leave town like the other poor weavers. Local weavers believed that if one could not make it in Kumbakonam, they could always make a good living in Kanchipuram. But, when the news started trickling in that even those weavers who had gone to Kanchipuram were now begging for food, he abandoned the idea of leaving town. His mother's savings were all but gone, and even her precious wedding chain had been pawned and their brass and bronze cooking pots sold. The situation was so dire that even a single meal a day seemed like good fortune, considering so many of them did not even have that, let alone any shelter.

It was a big surprise that even during these hard times, Saranathan not only stayed on with Kannan but also helped him. Saranathan's married life was very turbulent; he and his wife did not get along and often came to blows. One day, he beat her up badly, took her five-sovereign chain, pawned it for three hundred rupees and gave the money to Kannan. Kannan did not know what had transpired between Saranathan and his wife. He would not have accepted the money if he had known. He thought Saranathan had pawned his wife's jewellery only with her acquiescence. He grew increasingly closer to Saranathan.

'You're trusting our muthalali too much. Why is he giving money to everyone else but you? We're good with our hands and can survive wherever we go. We'll see better times only when we leave this muthalali,' said Saranathan often, trying to instigate Kannan.

'Yes, we're good with our hands. But, nowadays, that doesn't seem to command any respect! What can our muthalali do? We have our metal cups in our hands, and we are pawning them.

He has land and jewellery, and he is pawning them, that's all. We should be happy that he is providing us with a daily bowl of rice gruel at least. Times will change.'

'Since he seems pious, you have started trusting him. He had initially said he was going to give us ten rupees profit per sari, and after the fact, argued that it was only for nine-yard saris, robbing us of three hundred rupees that year. He must be making a profit of at least five thousand rupees per year from our work. Why can't he accommodate us during these hard times? He entertains himself by watching us starve. Is that fair? Does he eat any less? He still gets halva from Vengada Lodge.'

'Can everyone eat halva all the time? We, too, will get to eat it when the time is right. If we leave him now, it'll be our loss.'

'You are mistaken. We have not forgotten his help. But he should not forget our service either.'

'He has not forgotten. This is not the time to test him. As time passes, you will see.'

Even though Kannan could have left Ramasamy Iyer, he did not. Saranathan could have left Kannan but did not have the heart to do so either.

The days passed with plenty of misgivings and shortages.

## Chapter 9

The stagnation in the weaving industry finally began to lift as the national economy improved, with inflation coming close at its heel, which, in turn, increased the cash circulation. Earlier, only the wealthy wore silk saris, but now, everyone had money and eagerly took to wearing silk. In due course, silk production in Mysuru expanded to accommodate the boost in demand.

The silk industry raised its head again, and the saris that had been stockpiled due to a lack of demand during the stagnation rapidly sold at excellent prices. Manufacturers who had reduced the number of looms began to add new ones. Even the weavers who had left town started returning, and the Saurashtrian streets bustled with activity again. The hardship that they had all endured was quickly forgotten.

The life of the daily wage weavers became quite comfortable. They did not have to worry about any debts. As long as they made enough money to satisfy their hunger, life was good. But, contract weavers like Kannan were caught in a bind.

During the terrible shortages, Kannan had gradually accumulated loans, amounting to about one thousand and five hundred rupees. Impoverishment and distress were so overwhelming that he had not had the time to worry about his loans. Now that he was busy with work, the burden of his loans began to weigh upon him. He had no confidence of emerging from his debts. Sometimes, he even began to believe what the others said about his muthalali—Ramasamy Iyer had ruined him by extending him those loans.

The muthalali, popularly known as Mysore Ramasamy Iyer, was reputed among the weavers as someone who 'ruins you with loans. He enslaves you through his generosity.' Mysore, Giri, Jembu, Kulla and Konda are some of the popular family names among Saurashtrians. Usually, members belonging to the same gotra share a common family name.

Kannan's personal experience with his muthalali had been quite different. He owed almost nine hundred rupees to his muthalali. To him, it did not look like his muthalali was trying to keep him in debt. Kannan's cooperation to accommodate all of his muthalali's demands during hard times had earned him Ramasamy Iyer's affection. But, affection in the industry greatly depends on the market conditions. Expensive jari saris were in high demand; and since only experts like Kannan could weave them, the muthalali helped Kannan settle his loans. However, in the process, he made the exchange profitable for himself as well! He increased Kannan's contract looms from two to five. Earlier, had he not said that he would give ten rupees profit per nine-yard sari? Now, he agreed to pay that for six-yard sari too.

'Profits and losses are common in all vocations. If you're afraid, how will you progress? If you work hard, you'll be able to settle all your loans within a year and even put away some money,' his muthalali said encouragingly.

His muthalali's predictions came true. Two years sped by, and all of Kannan's outstanding loans were settled, including the one he owed to Saranathan, which he returned first. At the end of the second year, the muthalali owed him a thousand rupees.

The industry was thriving, and the weavers were being paid well. The muthalalis were focussed on expanding production. Wage employees demanded higher wages and issued strike notices twice. But, each time, there was no need for a strike, as representatives from both organizations came to an amicable agreement. The muthalalis accepted two of the four requests. Both parties were keen that there should not be any delays due to work stoppages.

Once he had a thousand rupees, Kannan was energized. His dream of a home of his own began to emerge again. There was a house available for rent on Thopu Street, for a deposit of a thousand rupees. The broker informed Kannan that it was a comfortable house and was for sale, if one was willing to pay an additional five hundred or seven hundred and fifty rupees. Kannan thought it would be best to purchase the house outright instead of paying a deposit and renting it. He told the broker that he would discuss the matter with his muthalali and return with his final decision. He broached the topic with his muthalali when he was in a good mood.

'Why this rush to buy a house? The current place is comfortable! I thought I could get you married,' his muthalali said.

'Why the rush to get me married now?'

'Your mother is growing old. Don't you need a woman to cook and take care of you?'

'My mother will live for another ten years. I've always wanted to own my own home, no matter how small it is, before I think of marriage. This has been a dream of mine for a long time, and I'm hoping that you'll help me fulfil it.'

His muthalali was consumed by his business those days, as he had suffered huge losses for three to four years during the economic downturn. He not only wanted to recover everything he had lost but also planned to double what he had before the bad times had hit him. His plans were being realized only with the cooperation and toil of expert weavers like Kannan. In the silk textile business, the profit margin increases with the amount of jari in a sari. Ramasamy Iyer found a way to increase the jari income by cheating. Genuine jari is made by rolling silver wire around a silk thread and casing it in gold. In competition with this genuine jari, the Surat traders produced brass jari at half the cost. Producers were reluctant to substitute this fake jari in silks, as they were concerned that it might undermine the value of their saris. But, Ramasamy Iyer dared to use fake jari and sell it as genuine jari. No one questioned him on the authenticity of the product, and therefore he did not have to lie to anyone. Due to his business 'acumen', when everyone else was making ten rupees profit on a sari, he was making twenty. This additional income was accumulating by the thousands as black money. White or black, a person is respected only when he possesses money.

He understood Kannan's desire to buy a home for himself. He also knew that he could continue to make a lot of money if he could keep Kannan tethered exclusively to his contracts.

'Have you told them that you're planning on purchasing the Thopu Street house?' Ramasamy Iyer asked Kannan.

'I have not said anything. They asked for a rental deposit. I told them I'll consult with you and let them know. Have I ever committed to anything without discussing it with you?' Kannan responded.

'Don't you like the house that you live in? Haven't many good things come your way after moving in there?'

'No complaints about the present house! Even if I buy a new house, I have no intentions of leaving this one.'

'If the present house becomes your own, would you like that?' laughed the muthalali, throwing a bombshell at him.

Kannan was startled. He stared blankly and mumbled, 'It's your house. How can it be mine?'

'You still don't seem to understand Mysore Ramasamy Iyer. He never fails to support those who depend on him,' he began his preamble boastfully. 'You have been with me for seven or eight years. Through thick and thin, you have stayed on. My wish is to see you as a family man. I'll sell you the house you currently live in for a small amount of money. Happy?'

*Am I happy!?* Kannan thought incredulously. His head was spinning. Mysore Ramasamy Iyer appeared like a god to him. What a big heart he had! He picked me up from the gutters and gave me a job and made me into a man. Now, he is willing to give me a house. Do even gods have such generous hearts?

'How would I have money to buy the house?' Kannan asked.

'I'll sell it to you for what you can afford to pay,' said his muthalali.

Kannan considered three thousand to be a reasonable amount. After deducting the thousand that his muthalali owed him, he would have an outstanding loan of two thousand. If he worked hard for two years, he could easily pay off that loan and make the house his own, Kannan calculated. He waited in anticipation to see how much his muthalali was going to propose.

'What use do I have from that house? You pay me twelve rupees a month as rent. Two months' rent goes towards taxes. When I repair the roof and fix up the house, what's left in it for me?'

'What are you going to gain by selling me the house?' asked Kannan, throwing an unnecessary spanner into the works.

'What am I going to gain out of it except the satisfaction of lighting a family lamp? How much were you planning on paying for the Thopu Street house?'

'It's a small place. They said I could get it for a thousand five hundred.'

'I'll give you my house for the same price, alright?'

Kannan could not believe what he heard.

'For a thousand five hundred? That's very...'

'Does it sound too high?'

'No! It just seems very low,' blabbered Kannan.

'You think I don't know that? Let it go! Live happily! I don't have any use for that house, and owning it seems to give you great joy. That in itself is enough for me. But, just one thing—times are changing. Everyone is forgetting the ones who helped them during times of need.'

'I'll never be one of them.'

'I'm going to write the house in your name in the hope that you'll not be one of them,' Ramasamy Iyer said and then, he started flipping the pages of the almanac and found an auspicious time to transfer the titles to Kannan.

Until Ramasamy Iyer signed on a stamp and registered the deeds in his name, Kannan was very uncertain. His dream came true, and now, he was the owner of a house—a really comfortable one! Such things do not come easy to a weaver, and he shared the news joyously with his mother. He also proudly announced it to Saranathan.

'Did you not repeatedly warn me not to trust Mysore—see what happened? If we keep moving over a loom or a muthalali, will we get a house like this?' Kannan asked.

'Did he give it away for free? We worked hard, and, as

a result, he made a lot of money. So, he gave you the house,' said Saranathan.

'Who else will give us one? It could be easily sold for three thousand rupees. By selling it he is not going to make a lot of money. There are so many of us weaving for him. Did everyone get this chance? You don't even have the heart to acknowledge those who help us!'

'I am not saying this is not help. I'm pointing out that there's also self-interest.'

'Our muthalali is not a mahatma to help without any self-interest. He, too, has children, relationships, likes and attachments, correct?'

Saranathan could not be at peace.

Kannan acquired the house.

How was Saranathan going to make peace with all this?

## Chapter 10

As soon as Kannan got legal ownership of his house, he went about making it clean and tidy: replaced the roof tiles, filled the holes on the floor with cement plaster and painted the walls with a homemade mix of paste and red ochre. He fenced in the two coconut trees that stood in his portion of the backyard, which were bearing fruit abundantly. He bought a small table and an almirah. Saranathan suggested that he should buy two chairs as well.

'There's still time for that,' said Kannan, dismissing his suggestion. He also bought two good-quality mats and decorated the electric lamps with fashionable shades. How beautiful the house looked now, as if Lakshmi had blessed it!

Kannan's friends were very happy to learn that he had bought his own house. He had a stream of visitors during the first few days, to all of whom he offered snacks and coffee. His status in his town seemed to have soared to new heights overnight.

Jembu Rangasamy was a jealous type. But, it was he who ultimately stopped Kannan from going overboard in beautifying the house. 'Yes, the house is yours now. But should you not be protecting it?' he asked.[18]

Kulla Krishnaiyan owned a small restaurant where Kannan had an account. Earlier, if the account balance went over five rupees, he would start nagging Kannan about it. But now, if Kannan merely sent word for some food for his ten or twelve guests, he would deliver it right away. Konda Veeraiyar, a lord Murugan devotee, advised Kannan to do an *abhisheka*[19] at Swamimalai[20]. Kannan was astonished by all the attention he was getting, and, at the same time, was enamoured by his new status in his community. The house sparkled. On top of all this, Saranathan began calling him muthalali. Once Saranathan started, the other four weavers working for Kannan followed suit.

'What's this? All of a sudden you're calling me muthalali?' Kannan chastised Saranathan while feeling quite thrilled.

'When someone runs a business with money inherited from his forefathers, we call them muthalali. When someone makes money by pandering to the powerful and oppressing the working class, we call them muthalali. You have made it with your own toil and sweat. It's only right that you are called a muthalali. No

---

[18] It is insinuated that making the house look beautiful might lead someone to cast an evil eye on it.
[19] Purification or cleansing ceremony done at a temple
[20] A famous Murugan temple near Kumbakonam

matter what you say, I will call you that!' Saranathan declared loudly, in the presence of four witnesses.

'Once I make it in life, you can call me that,' protested Kannan softly—not wanting anyone else to hear him.

'Do you want to own your own looms? Just say so, and I'll make arrangements with the jari and silk stores!' said Saranathan, further raising Kannan's hopes.

Succumbing to Saranathan's pressure, Kannan bought good shirts and expensive eight-mulam veshtis.[21] He also bought a few for Saranathan. He did not forget his mother either. He got her a couple of cotton saris. In short, homeownership landed him in debt again. But, this time, he felt confident that he would be able to settle them without too much trouble. Once again, he was working very hard and encouraged Saranathan and the others to do so as well.

He got used to being referred to as muthalali. But he was not satisfied to stop at a mere title. None of his family members had ever owned a home. They had always lived in shared rented houses with five or six other families. Quite often, they had to pick up their pots and pans and move to another dwelling when things did not work out. He had wanted to own a home and that had finally happened.

Similarly, should he not own his looms and become a minor muthalali? Weavers very rarely ended up as muthalalis—only a few had ever reached those heights. Nannapiyer had once been

---

[21] Usually worn by upper class men, as they are more expensive

a daily wage weaver, but now, he owned forty to fifty looms. Kannan wondered why he could not become like Nannapiyer, as there were no laws stopping him. As long as he worked diligently and hard, there was nothing that was going to stop him from reaching his goals.

Mysore Ramasamy Iyer was fond of Kannan, and, with his support, he could definitely advance in life. Kannan had obtained five contract looms from him, and, in a year, he was able to weave at least two hundred six-yard saris—the profit alone amounted to two thousand rupees. He was able to save on wages as well. Within two years, he could save enough capital to purchase four or five looms. If you work hard, is anything beyond reach?

Kannan was not a pipe dreamer. His hard work was the foundation for his capital; he toiled tirelessly. The weavers who wove for him were also good workers, and he compensated them fairly for their hard work. So, they, too, put their hearts and souls into their work.

Kannan was driven by his obsession to become a muthalali, not just in title. Earlier, he would go to the movie theatre to watch every new release, but now, he completely abandoned that habit. He would weave all day and then continue until midnight. Saranathan was weaving on one of the looms in Kannan's house. He tried competing with Kannan but could not keep up with him. Saranathan was afflicted by the early stages of elephantiasis. Weaving on the loom put a great strain on the legs all day, and this posture caused Saranathan to develop swollen lymph nodes. He had frequent bouts of fever. Kannan had to stop him from weaving at night.

Saranathan was taking care of Kannan's finances. He was very competent at both weaving as well as maintaining accounts. Kannan was very grateful for the friendship and support that he received from Saranathan and completely trusted his bookkeeping.

Kannan was succeeding in life. While his mother was growing older, she looked younger by the day. Although she had once looked withered, she now looked hale and hearty. She had never had such a comfortable life. The sense of peace that she enjoyed now showed on her figure. But, she was not lazy and did all the housework while helping with the looms too. She also made yarn for the other manufacturers for wages. Her son gave her sufficient money to cover their household expenses, and she managed to save a part of it. He also gave her money for her visits to the temples and films, and she saved some of that as well. So, she accumulated money from various sources, and the more money that came her way, the more obsessed she became with it.

She often nagged Kannan to get married. Although she enjoyed all the comforts, she felt she was deprived of one thing in life: she did not have a daughter-in-law to boss over. She kept mumbling, 'How nice it would be to have a married woman in the house and to enjoy watching tots running around!' This constant muttering became an annoyance for Kannan.

Only one of her three daughters was married in

Kumbakonam and lived nearby. The other two resided out of town, but her two elder sons also lived in the same town as her. They had all been disrespectful to her in the past, but she forgot all that. She started visiting them without Kannan's knowledge. Perhaps she longed to show off how comfortable her life was now. She continued to visit them, even after Kannan found out. Then, her grandchildren began staying with her for a few days each time they visited. Kannan did not attempt to stop any of this. He happily welcomed them. He just wanted his mother to be happy.

Do magnets even have as much power as money? Now, both his elder brothers and their wives began visiting Kannan, exercising their rediscovered kinship. Their visits meant more expenses, beginning with feeding them during their stays and ending with making special food items to send along with them when they returned home. Kannan's mother prepared many dishes during their visits. Where did his mother get the energy to labour all day?

Kannan did not have the time to worry about these additional expenses or to figure out how to economize on their household expenses. Ramasamy Iyer had increased his contract looms to ten, and Kannan barely had time to manage them. In addition, he had his own weaving to attend to. Saranathan had to cope with the additional accounting work for which Kannan increased his salary. He worked cheerfully, and the income kept pouring in. Kannan thought of this as a dress rehearsal for becoming a real muthalali. In this situation, he did not bother about his mother's merriment and entertainment.

But, one day, after dinner, his mother took up the matter. 'Your brothers are like cheap currency, we see them all the time. You have forgotten your younger sister. The elder two are not in town, we can see them sometime later. But, how can we forget the one who lives right by us?' she asked subtly.

'Everyone is visiting freely, she can too. Did I ever say that she couldn't?' Kannan retorted.

'How can she come here just like that? Your brothers didn't think twice about it. But can your younger sister do the same? You'll have to formally invite her and her husband to come here.'

'Is her husband refusing to send her here?'

'How will he send her here? Did you invite them? All of you got her married and sent her off! Then, which one of you bothered to see how she was doing?'

'Amma, I'm the youngest son. When I have older brothers, what can *I* do?'

'The elder two can barely feed themselves. How can they afford to invite her? By god's grace, you're doing well. So, you should invite her and her husband over for a feast.'

He did not see anything wrong with what his mother was saying. He definitely felt that forgetting his sister was not right. He decided to invite his sister, Subathrai, and her husband over.

'Alright, Amma, I'll go over to their house and bring them back with me.'

'Just because you invited them, are they going to come running?'

'What are you saying?' asked Kannan, quite confused.

'What else? After she was married off, did you at least invite her over for a single meal? Even on special holidays you didn't bother to look her up. Earlier, when you didn't have the means, you couldn't do anything for her. Let's put that behind us. What do you lack now?'

It had been a long time since he had heard his mother speak so harshly and for the first time after moving out with him.

'Amma, I have already told you that I'll invite them over!'

'When I am here, an elder in the house, how can you invite them? I invited my son-in-law. "Even when you bought the house, did you bother to invite us over for the housewarming? What business do I have in your house now?" he said to me. He has a point. Were you not serving food and coffee to everyone who stopped by our house? Did you even think of your younger sister then?'

Kannan understood that his mother was aiming for something big. 'Just let me know what I should do. You're the elder in this house, and whatever you say is good with me. I'm getting sleepy now.'

'Even as an elder I have not been fortunate. I don't have the privilege of even inviting my daughter for a meal.'

'Who told you not to invite her over?'

The argument did not budge from where it had begun. Kannan had been working all day, and now his eyelids were heavy with sleep. He wanted to put an end to this conversation. 'Tomorrow is Friday. Saturday and Sunday are not good days. On Monday, after the *Rahu* period[22] ends, you and I can visit them and invite your son-in-law, all right?'

'He will not come here,' Kannan's mother answered coldly.

'If we invite him politely, he will. It all depends on our tone.'

'If we merely invite him, he'll not come. When I invited him, he said that they will come only if we give him two hundred rupees for all the wrongs we have committed in the past.'

The riddle was solved. Kannan understood now.

The son-in-law status itself bestows arrogance, right? The arrogance of Brahmin sons-in-law is infamous, but Saurashtrian sons-in-law put the Brahmin ones to shame. When they get married, there are rules about jewellery and dowry received from the bride. An educated groom has a rate; if he has an important job then another rate. Even now, overcoming these hurdles is a huge burden for the bride's parents, and the obligations persist even after the wedding. For the first year following the wedding, the bride's family has to provide elaborate meals to the groom's family on special days. Deepavali requires the bride's family to buy new clothes for the groom. For a year or six months following the wedding, it is customary that the bride's family will provide all the groom's meals. Do you really think that the groom is going to come over of his own volition and have a meal at the bride's family house? Would that not degrade

---

[22]The Rahu period is considered bad timing in Hindu astrology.

the groom's superior status? The groom has to be invited and escorted by the bride's brother or some other relative to enjoy the meal. The groom might live on the adjacent street, but a vehicle must be sent to bring him! All these conventions apply to the local grooms. Then, what about grooms who live out of town? You need to gift him money to compensate for everything that he missed out on. One blunder in providing the meals and gifts could end up costing you a penalty of five rupees to a thousand, and only after shelling this out would the bride and groom visit you.

This is what Kannan's mother was implying. Usually, mothers tend to love their daughters more than their sons. Kannan's mother felt that Kannan was doing well, and yet, had not treated her son-in-law according to convention. So, she believed paying a two-hundred-rupee penalty and inviting them was a good idea.

Kannan had not reached a stage in life where he could consider two hundred rupees to be a trivial amount. If this amount had to be spent in small increments, he might not have cared as much. But, when a penalty of two hundred rupees was mentioned, Kannan's drowsiness vanished. He was the youngest son of the house. His elder brothers should have taken care of all their duties towards their youngest sister. Does the groom not know that he had left his family's house with only the clothes on his back? Just like his brothers, even the groom did not care about him then. Kannan was willing to let go of the past and invite his brother-in-law, but he was not prepared to pay a financial penalty for that. This was his stance.

His mother got tired of repeating her position on this matter. She did not verbally blame Kannan for making her look detestable in the eyes of her daughters but instead began wailing, beating her chest and stomach. She had a loud voice, and their house was adjacent to the street. The commotion in Kannan's house attracted a crowd of neighbours. Some knocked on the door and called out to him. He had been socializing with others in a very respectable manner, and her wailing was humiliating. He stepped outside the house and told his neighbours that his mother was weeping thinking of his late father and dispersed the crowd!

Later, he could not stop her lament. Once his mother realized that Kannan was worried about what others might think of her weeping, her wailing became even louder. Kannan's patience was being tested. He truly wanted his mother to have a peaceful life. But once she started becoming belligerent, he was tempted to slap her and shut her up. He attempted to control his anger and tried to fall asleep. How is one supposed to fall asleep in this commotion? He pretended to sleep. His mother finally abandoned her wailing, believing he had fallen asleep and fell asleep herself.

However, his mother's resistance did not abate. The next day, she prepared their meals as usual, but she did not eat or speak to her son. She was silent and refused to respond to his questions. He was afraid that she might start wailing again. When she skipped dinner and began starving herself, he felt miserable. He did not have the heart to pay two hundred rupees and appease his brother-in-law, but neither did he have the guts to prolong the standoff with his mother. Saranathan found out that the mother and son had quarrelled and became the self-appointed mediator. He could not find a way to pacify Kannan's mother, so he reprimanded Kannan. He argued that one had to go along with social conventions, and that it was only right to pay the two hundred rupees and invite his sister and brother-in-law. Seeing no other way out, Kannan agreed to this arrangement. Even after this decision, Saranathan had to sit beside Kannan's mother and cajole her to give up her hunger strike!

The path was cleared, and now, along with his brothers, his younger sister and her husband began visiting them. His house was always busy with people and feasts. All his siblings and family were poor. So, when they saw glue, they attached themselves to it. Kannan's household expenses began to rise steeply!

His financial burden did not stop with the additional entertainment expenses. He noticed that, without his knowledge, sundry items were also being taken by his siblings. He suffered, unable to either ignore or swallow these incidents. He did not have the courage to take on his mother, and his weaving obligations did not permit him the time to dwell on it either. Since he had sufficient income, he did not worry about it for too long.

His mother's irresponsible behaviour only worsened with

time as her age caught up with her. The fear that she might die any time soon gripped her. She felt she had to settle all her debts before passing away, at least to God if not to other human beings.

When Kannan was five years old, he had a bout of high fever—there had been little hope of him surviving it. Even the doctors had given up hope. At that time, his mother had made a vow to visit the Tirupati temple and shave her hair off as penance if Kannan were to survive his illness. She did not remember that 'request' at all, but her elder son, Murthy, reminded her of it at a convenient time.

It seemed like God himself had waited for him to remind his mother! Soon after, God started appearing in her dreams and frightening her! She frequently told Kannan of her promise and nagged him about visiting Tirupati. Kannan, too, liked the idea but was afraid it might get in the way of his work commitments. He was also worried about the ensuing expenses. But, a Tirupati visit became an obsession with his mother, and her request did not seem unreasonable to Kannan. As usual, she began scolding Kannan and lamenting about it to everyone who visited her. Her elder son also intervened, insisting that Kannan should take their mother to Tirupati.

Kannan agreed half-heartedly. His assent was all that was needed from him. All the arrangements were taken care of right away. Kannan was astounded when he found out how elaborate the pilgrimage was going to be. It seemed like you could have a wedding in all that preparation! His elder brother and family camped out at his house. Before one embarks on a pilgrimage, one has to wear yellow clothes and perform the ritual of asking for alms in town, accompanied by drummers and musicians. Since Kannan was not married yet, his elder brother and wife had to perform all these rituals. One also has to get permission from the son-in-law. Some suggested to Kannan, 'It is only right that you take your sister and her husband along,' and his mother jumped at the idea! In the end, the pilgrimage included Kannan's elder brother and family, his second sister-in-law and her two children, his younger sister and family—a total of sixteen tickets to travel!

Kannan could not talk back. Except for money, no one expected anything else from him. Even his muthalali hesitated when Kannan told him about the impending visit to Tirupati, not wanting him to leave when he was so busy with work. When he realized that Kannan was drowning in familial obligations, he lent him two thousand rupees.

Saranathan agreed to take on the work responsibilities while Kannan was away. Everything went well. Kannan left for Tirupati along with his 'family'.

But, the pilgrimage did not end with Tirupati. The list expanded to Tiruvannamalai, Tiruttani, Thirukalukundram, Chennai, Kanchipuram and so on. By the time they returned home, twenty-five days had passed. Not only had the two thousand rupees been spent, but Kannan also had to write to his muthalali and request another three hundred rupees to return home.

Kannan was happy for the opportunity to worship Lord Venkadachalapathy in peace. When he finally mentally calculated all the expenses and the losses due to the work he had forgone, even he, courageous as he was, was petrified. Only after offsetting all these losses could he rise again!

Saranathan took care of the accounting as usual. When Kannan settled his accounts with his muthalali at the end of the year, there was a shortfall in the weight of silk and jari; about a thousand rupees had disappeared. This was an additional loss, on top of the Tirupati expenses.

Saranathan argued that Ramasamy Iyer had cheated Kannan, taking advantage of his gullible nature, while his muthalali chastised Kannan for being an extravagant spender and being 'ruined' by associating with untrustworthy people. Of the two, Kannan did not know whom to suspect—both seemed very honest. He could not understand how a thousand rupees had vanished into thin air.

## Chapter 11

*Let bygones be bygones! I will be vigilant going forward,* Kannan vowed to himself. *My income and expenses have ballooned, and if one keeps worrying about the past then the present is going to be wasted,* he concluded. So, at night, after Saranathan left for the day, he reviewed his daily accounts.

He could not economize on his household expenses. On the one hand, he could not control his mother's spending habits, and on the other, he could not limit his expenses either. Since the pilgrimage, his elder brother had become very close to him. He didn't fail to demand whatever he needed from Kannan, taking advantage of his fraternal relationship, since he had a big family with a lot of needs. Kannan did not have the strength to refuse his continual demands.

Seven or eight months after returning from their Tirupati pilgrimage, his mother started running a fever. She took some local remedies for a few days. Then, suddenly, she lost consciousness and passed away shortly after.

As soon as the old woman fell ill, people started thronging his house. When she passed away, his brothers and their families arrived, as it was the sons' duty to perform the last rites. His younger sister and her husband as well as the two out-of-town sisters came as soon as the news reached them.

Kannan was grief-stricken by his mother's death. He did not worry about the expenses and wanted to conduct the funeral grandly. But, while the body was still in repose, a serious disagreement arose among the family members.

At the time of her death, the old woman had been wearing a four-sovereign necklace, bangles of two sovereigns each and a pair of new diamond earrings. Kannan had gotten them made for her, anticipating that they might help him during times of financial hardship. Conflict arose over this jewellery; the daughters argued that their mother's jewellery rightfully belonged to them, and the sons argued that the daughters-in-law had the right to a share as well. Verbal arguments heated up, with the women on the verge of coming to blows with each other. 'These are mine', muttered Kannan but was not heard by anyone. Condolers at the funeral had to make peace between the daughters and the daughters-in-law.

It was finally decided that fighting amongst themselves while the body was still in the house was not right. They concluded that her jewellery and money box should be given to a mediator, whose decision, to be made the day after the funeral, would be binding. Everyone agreed to nominate Jembu Rangasamy as the mediator, who said that the jewellery might be removed before the cremation but the money box was to be locked and handed over to him. Everyone expected to see a hundred or two hundred rupees in the box. But, the box was already open—there was an old silver coin and a few half and quarter anna coins in it. Kannan was stunned. Obviously, someone had opened the box. Who could have done this? Everyone had a free rein of the house. But, all of Kannan's siblings suspected him! The two sisters, who had arrived from out of town, lamented that their brother would die of diarrhoea for his deceit.

Only after it was decided that the mediation should be limited to the jewellery did the last rites begin.

Kannan was dumbfounded and did not know what to cry about. The relatives who had disappeared during his hard times were now fighting over the division of the cash. He was disgusted and ashamed. Each one of them knew that their mother's jewellery was entirely the fruit of Kannan's hard labour, and yet, no one was willing to take that into consideration. *It's all for the better. I'll never see them again. Just let Amma's funeral get over*, he grumbled to himself.

The mediation transpired as he had expected. Even though Jembu Rangasamy was Kannan's friend, he said that just because the jewellery had been Kannan's gift to his mother, it was not his property. 'The daughters and daughters-in-law should get equal shares,' was his final decision, and he divided the jewellery up. Only then did the fighting end.

On the thirteenth day after the funeral, the spiritual

impurities are warded off and auspiciousness is ushered in. All the siblings and their families stayed at Kannan's house until then. Somehow or the other, all matters were taken care of. Kannan's eldest brother told him that he could move into Kannan's house with his family and could help Kannan out. But he firmly told his brother that he did not need anyone's help and that he was quite capable of cooking and taking care of himself. After everyone returned to their own homes, Saranathan told Kannan that the total funeral expenses had amounted to seven hundred and fifty rupees.

'That is not the end of it. The lost jewellery amounts to about eight hundred rupees; pots and pans worth about seventy to eighty rupees are also missing. Add all that up and see!' said Kannan, emotionally exhausted.

## Chapter 12

Kannan began cooking for himself, and since he lived alone, he was able to eat whatever appealed to him. More than the cooking, the real nuisance was the house cleaning and washing the cooking vessels, with burnt food stuck to the bottom, for which he hired a cleaning woman. Nevertheless, without a woman, the house lost its glow and was dreary.

Until his mother had been alive, she had harassed Kannan to get married, and his muthalali kept at it as well. After his mother's death, the muthalali's nagging intensified, but he praised Kannan for cutting off ties with his siblings over the disputed jewellery. Further, he advised Kannan that if he wanted to become a responsible person and have passion in life, he had to surrender himself to a wife.

Kannan was thirty, and men of his age already had three or four children. He finally began to feel the need for a woman, both physically and emotionally. It was not that he had had no interest in women or in getting married, but his preoccupation with money had overshadowed everything else in life.

Kannan cared a lot about his physical well-being. Dyeing silk thread and weaving were tasks that strengthened one's physique, but some aspects of his work were harmful to his well-being. The youth in his neighbourhood had established the Hanuman Exercise Club, furnished it with various exercise equipment and had even hired a coach to train them. Young men got together in the mornings and evenings and exercised there. Kannan usually exercised in the evenings for at least half an hour. In the beginning, he aspired to compete in bodybuilding competitions but soon realized that it would take up all his time, and physical workouts were already getting in the way of his weaving. Therefore, he exercised moderately to maintain his health, and thus his body was as strong as his mind.

Chatting with his friends and going to the films kindled the desire for a wife in him. His nights were disturbed when women appeared in his dreams. Sometimes, even during the day, he would stare at women in a daze, agonizing all the while. Frequently, when women looked at him, he was utterly confused. His unrelenting resolve to accumulate money and acquire his own loom before giving in to these desires had won over his mind. Even though, at times, his body resisted against this resolve, ultimately, he was able to pacify his urges.

After his mother's demise, even his interest in material things seemed to dim. He could not make sense of the longing that engulfed him, and in the beginning, he thought that it was the grief of losing his mother that was causing these confusing emotions. Given her advancing age, her death had been expected, and soon enough, he realized that this was not what was causing his emotional turmoil. Even though he encouraged the other weavers to work hard, he felt sluggish and without any zeal. He became indifferent toward everything and felt his body getting weaker. When he came across women, he felt a distinct giddiness. It did not take long for him to realize that his body was yearning for a union. He felt he was separate from his body, and, at times, he even feared that his body might get out of control and do something wrong.

Then, there was some good news! He heard about Padmanabha Iyer's daughter, Kausalai, of Thuvarankurichi South Street. She was beautiful and did all the housework and cooking with charming perfection, and it was said that she knew matters related to weaving as well. Padmanabha Iyer had also heard about Kannan, obtained Kannan's horoscope from his eldest brother and already consulted an astrologer, who confirmed that the horoscopes matched. Kannan's eldest brother brought news that Padmanabha Iyer was prepared to give his daughter to Kannan and advised him to see her when he went to the river to fetch water.

Kannan did not put on any airs. One evening, when Kausalai was at the river with her friends, he went to see her. Since she did not know that Kannan was there to observe her, she was her usual self, laughing and enjoying herself with her friends. To say that Kannan liked her as soon as he saw her would be an understatement; a new emotion exploded within him. He felt like he would be unable to eat anything unless it was served by her. He even ran a slight fever that night.

Both parties liked the alliance. The wedding matters were handled according to custom and arranged by his eldest brother. The bride's father agreed to gift his daughter with a six-sovereign necklace, a pair of earrings, a few gold bangles and silver *kolusu*[23]. Instead of occasionally providing food for the groom during the week, Padmanabha Iyer gave Kannan two hundred rupees and another three hundred rupees for the *shanthi muhurtham*[24]. For all other obligations that were due to the groom, the bride's father agreed to act according to local conventions. Padmanabha Iyer was a weaver who owned ten weaving looms, which he had acquired through his hard work. Therefore, he wanted to spend lavishly on his daughter's wedding. He gave a hundred rupees to Kannan's elder brother for arranging the marriage. Kannan was not going to be outspent by his father-in-law and gifted an equal amount of jewellery to his future wife.

The wedding celebrations were unlike a typical weaver's wedding. They were ostentatious and grand, like a middle-class marriage. Some muthalalis, including Mysore Ramasamy Iyer,

---

[23] Anklets
[24] The consummation of the marriage

and labour union leaders also attended the wedding. The expenses far exceeded Kannan's budget, but all this just made him happy.

## Chapter 13

Kannan was a bridegroom now. The Saurashtrians of the Thuvarankurichi area in Kumbakonam being sticklers for following traditions, Kannan's father-in-law provided his meals for the first six months. The wedding took place in May and the shanthi muhurtham was to be held in August. Kannan was as fat as a bull now. Kausalai would sometimes serve him food at his father-in-law's house; after the shanthi muhurtham, she went back and forth between Kannan's and her father's houses.

Kausalai was very fair-skinned, slim but firmly built. The newlyweds explored the secrets of their bodies with enthusiasm, limitlessly. Is there any point in finding the horizon of one's ecstasy? It was perfectly obvious that Kausalai had to merely move her little finger and Kannan would be dancing to her tune. While he was not afraid of his wife, he was definitely under her control.

It was generally believed that in such female-dominated families things went awry, but Kausalai was a very smart woman. She understood that her family comprised Kannan and herself. She detached herself from her husband's family smoothly. Remarkably, she did this so shrewdly that no one held a grudge against her. She made sure that she and Kannan benefited from her parents and siblings. Her policy was simple: 'What will you bring us when you visit us? What will you give us when we visit you?'

She counted on her father to enforce this policy. He had four sons, but she was his only daughter, and he loved her dearly. He was astonished at how well his little sparrow ran her household and he visited his son-in-law's house often.

He did not like that Kannan was still being controlled by his muthalali. He wanted Kannan to own four looms—an aspiration Kausalai shared. Kannan never tried to hide anything from his father-in-law, and, together, they would go over the accounts. Fifteen months after their wedding, the burden of Kannan's debt did not seem to decrease. He tried to let his father-in-law know that it was not going to be possible to acquire his own looms while paying off his debts. His father-in-law was uneasy about this situation.

During this time, there had been a big transformation in Ramasamy Iyer's household. The muthalali had a stroke and became partially paralysed. His two sons took over the administrative responsibilities of his business. Belonging to an unemotional and younger generation, they believed that their father's generosity had led to a lot of waste. They took a stern line with their weavers. They refused to pay anything over the wages and resorted to harsh tactics to recover the monies their father had loaned to the weavers.

They were not lenient with Kannan either, particularly because they knew of his influence over their father. They believed that he had enjoyed too many privileges and that his contract looms were a financial loss to them. All in all, they treated Kannan harshly and with contempt.

By then, Kannan had changed from the days when he had roamed around like a refugee, with only the clothes on his back. Ten weavers called him muthalali now, and he had a wife at home to rule over. The scorn of the younger muthalalis began to bother him. He was still grateful to his old muthalali, but he was a unique individual, wasn't he?

Kausalai and her father understood Kannan's dilemma. Pathmanabha Iyer had a lot of experience in these matters; he stood by his son-in-law and watched over him. He advised Kannan to give up the ten contract looms and to get two or three of his own looms. The goal was to slowly increase the number of looms that he owned. Saranathan welcomed this idea warmly.

Their plans came to fruition within six to seven months. Kannan had a balance of five hundred rupees, owing to the younger muthalalis, and even they agreed that Kannan could pay it off in small amounts.

Kannan's father-in-law quickly started making alternate arrangements for him. He took a loan of a thousand rupees for

Kannan by placing a lien on Kannan's house. He also secured five hundred rupees worth of silk yarn and jari for Kannan on loans from the shops that he patronized.

When all the weavers left, Kannan's house was silent. It was true that he was in debt now, but his lifelong dream had finally come true. He now owned two looms. Both were of the kind that wove big jari and were placed in his house. He wove on one and Saranathan on the other. Kausalai helped out with all the additional work related to both the looms. In the beginning, they thought she could weave on the second loom. But, she was not familiar with 'big' weaves, and Kannan did not like the idea of her weaving.

The day Kannan set up his independent business, his father-in-law blessed him heartily: 'Son-in-law, don't lose hope. Even a big house is built one stone at a time. It's not going to be long before the two looms become twenty!'

Everything seemed to be going well for Kannan. His wife's attentive looks and touches made him stronger. He worked very hard day and night. As soon as he completed a sari, his father-in-law sold it for a good price and gave him cash for it. Kausalai also got pregnant during this time.

Even though Kausalai had the gift of the gab, she was not combative and was affable towards everyone. Her daily routine included going to the river to wash clothes and bathe in the mornings. There, she got to know Hema. Who can tell how friendship blossoms between two women? Hema was socially superior to Kausalai, but Kausalai's looks had a certain elegance that went beyond status. Perhaps, this was what Hema had been drawn to.

Their friendship, which began by the riverside, deepened by the day. Hema visited Kausalai once in a while, whereas Kausalai visited Hema regularly; if they wanted to go to the cinema, temple or shops, they did so together. While Kausalai was in labour, Hema was by her side the entire time, and when Kausalai delivered a baby girl, Hema was overjoyed. For all the closeness to Kausalai, Hema had never once looked Kannan in the eye nor spoken to him.

'Lakshmi has arrived. While she was still in your womb, a new business was underway. As time goes by, great things are going to happen!' said Hema, making Kausalai very happy.

Kannan finally experienced the satisfaction of enjoying all-round happiness in life. He had become a weaver at fourteen; about eighteen years later, he was still a weaver. But, now, he was in a much better place in life—he owned a home and had a wife, a baby and two looms. No average weaver attained these milestones easily. Kannan was now hopeful that his future was going to be even better.

While his debt continued to burden him as if it was saying, 'I'm going to swallow everything you have,' his physical strength countered, 'I'll resist and absorb anything thrown at me.'

The rain seemed to have descended to aid his monstrous debt, unleashing immensely cruel times.

## Chapter 14

Kannan couldn't understand why Hema had asked to speak to him now, when she had rushed away each time their paths had crossed in the past. He worried about whether she was asking to speak to him about her own family matters.

Kannan usually mingled easily with women of his own status. But, all that had begun to change after he became the owner of his house and two looms. Some women from poorer households started respecting him, and even a few wealthy women began to notice him. But, as far as he was concerned, he was still a weaver. Even though he was happy to be called a muthalali, he found it difficult to act like one and was still embarrassed to speak to women of a higher social class.

Kannan knew Hema's history, although briefly. She was the younger sister of the silk fabric manufacturer Rajagopal Iyer of Middle Street. He owned about fifty looms and moved in the circles of powerful muthalalis. Hema had been married into a well-to-do family but had not been fortunate enough to have really lived with her husband, who was from Ayyampettai; even their shanthi muhurtham had not happened. Once or twice, when Hema had served him food at her father's house, he had grabbed her hands and flirted, but nothing more. During one of his visits to his father-in-law's house, he had gone to bathe in Arasalar River and drowned in a flood despite being a good swimmer.

Thus, the sun of Hema's marital life had set even before it rose. It was common knowledge that her husband's family had compensated her with twenty thousand rupees for breaking her *thaali*[25]. She had only been twenty when she became a widow. Her brother and his family were kind to her, feeling sorry that she had lost all happiness at a very young age. Because she came with money, this kindness gave her independence as well. She was housebound for about two years after the tragedy, but after that, she started moving about wherever she pleased. You could see her at the cinema on the first day of any movie or seated in the front row at temple festivals. Usually, such women were the topic of a lot of gossip, and Hema was no exception. Kannan had heard it too, but Kausalai had a very high opinion of her. Beyond that, he did not pay much attention to Hema.

---

[25]Thaali is a small gold pendant fastened around the bride's neck during the wedding ceremony by the groom. When a woman becomes a widow, it is removed by her husband's family to indicate her widowhood.

'Kausalai! Why did you call me?' asked Kannan as he entered the kitchen. His instincts warned him that it was best to speak to her in this manner.

'Hema called you! She wants to speak to you about something,' Kausalai responded.

'With me?'

'I'm the one who asked to speak to you,' said Hema, breaking her silence. As soon as Kannan entered the kitchen, she stood up with Kausalai's baby on her hips. 'Kausalai told me that your warp and jari got drenched. She is worried about the losses caused by the rain.'

'So what? If I work hard for four days, it'll all even out,' Kannan responded.

'How many days are you going to continue like this? Now you have a baby as well.'

Kannan assumed that Hema was talking to him with her head bowed, as he, too, had his eyes on the floor. The compassion in her voice and the empathy she showed towards his family's welfare surprised him. He looked up at her. When one saw Hema for the first time, no one would guess that she was a widow; there was no kumkum on her forehead, but her powdered face was very beautiful. With diamond earrings, three of four necklaces, a nose ring, six-sovereign bangles, wearing a silk sari and silk blouse, she did not look like someone who was grieving. He did not understand why she was so worried about their sad plight.

'Tell him, Hema!' said Kausalai, prompting her.

'I have three thousand rupees. My elder brother does not

know about it, only my mother does. I will lend you that money. You can use it to expand your business—just give me a small share of the profits. I, too, have no support. How long is my brother going to support me? I don't get along with my sister-in-law and we fight every day. I gave everything I had to my brother and am now utterly dependent on him. I wanted to give it to you for safe keeping. If I have the backing of a person like you, I too, will feel confident,' blurted Hema.

Kannan noticed that her voice was quivering. He had never expected such a proposition from her. Three thousand rupees! He was not concerned about the amount. After all, he had spent that amount for a Tirupati pilgrimage. But it seemed like a huge sum now that there was a lien on his house, the rains had damaged his wares and silk and jari owners had lent him money with stipulations. If he had three thousand rupees now, he could do a lot of things. But, the way in which it was offered did not seem right. On the contrary, he sensed danger. Hema was a widow from a well-to-do household, so taking her money without anyone else's knowledge seemed improper.

'*Neenga sollra sari*,'[26] said Kannan speaking directly to her.

'You keep referring to me as "*neenga neenga*"; I am, after all...er...am I not younger than you?'

'You're right,' he said and hesitated to go on.

'Why can't we do as Hema says? It will be good for us

---

[26]This phrase means 'what you are saying is right'. Kannan uses the word 'neenga', a respectful way to address an elder or a person of a higher socio-economic status.

as well as her,' interjected Kausalai. Her only concern at that point was to secure some money, and Kannan's hesitation annoyed her.

'If her brother finds out about it tomorrow, what do you think will happen? It will create unnecessary displeasure,' Kannan retorted.

'My brother is going to find out only if I tell him, right? I promise you, I will not let anyone else know about this,' said Hema.

Kausalai came to Hema's defence: 'Why is she going to tell anyone? We are not going to let her down. We can buy four looms and pay ourselves wages for our hard work; we can pay her interest on her investment. Then, we can split whatever is left between us. Does that sound good, Hema?'

'I keep saying I am for it. But I can't understand why he is so reluctant to take it. I am giving it wholeheartedly, what else is there to it?' Hema asked.

Kannan understood his wife's intentions. She knew her husband could perform 'miracles' with the three thousand rupees, but what he could not understand was why Hema was persuading him to take her money when their acquaintance was so recent and limited.

'Let's think about it before we proceed,' he said.

'What's there to think about? Just say yes! I have given the money to Rangaiyer's household to earn interest. If I want the money back, I need to give him ten days' notice,' said Hema.

Kausalai inquired: 'Will they be able to give you the entire three thousand in one instalment?'

'Is that a big amount for them? If Kannan gives me the nod, I can go there this evening and let them know,' Hema responded.

'Why does he need to give you the nod? Instead, I will give you a resounding nod. You can let them know this evening!' Kausalai said, and both the women smiled at each other. It seemed that they had come to a mutually satisfactory decision.

Kannan, however, was still not clear about the matter. 'Don't do anything in a hurry. You should think about it carefully. Kausalai and I will discuss the matter and will let you know.'

'I came here only after thinking this matter through carefully. Please don't think of me as a stranger. I'm your woman. If you let me down, I have nobody else,' Hema pleaded. Her voice faltered as she spoke and she wiped her eyes. Her language further confused Kannan—he was dumbfounded. Hema was a wealthy woman. Her elder brother was an influential man. The talk of the town was that her younger brother was going to marry into a rich family. Her mother was also quite well off. With all this, why was she saying that she was depending on *him*?

Tears were streaming down Hema's eyes, and she kept wiping them. It seemed as if her tears would stop only after handing the three thousand rupees over to Kannan.

'Now, why are you crying? Who is he going to consult on this matter? Me, right? And I'm on your side! You don't need to worry about anything. We will not let you down,' Kausalai consoled Hema.

'Amma! Is muthalali not there?' someone called from outside.

'Kaakaasuran[27] is here. You can leave now and attend to him,' Kausalai instructed her husband.

---

[27]Kausalai's nickname for Saranathan because he was dark like a crow

## Chapter 15

'Muthalali, when the whole town is flooded, how can you sit and chat so calmly?' Saranathan demanded of Kannan.

'What else do you expect me to do? I have already rolled up both the looms and feel as if I have live embers tied around my stomach. Rangan came over earlier, and we unrolled the warps. The jari looks like it is going to take a lot of work. Shall we clean up the warps?' Kannan responded.

'First we have to prepare food for the dead. It is raining heavily, there seems to be no end to the monster's revolt. Last night I left here around nine, right? I rushed back home because I was very hungry. The cat was guarding the kitchen and my wife was curled up fast asleep. I woke her up and asked, "Aren't you cooking?" "No kerosene; how to light the stove?" she answers back!'

'Should you not give her some money?' Kannan asked.

'Of course, I did. Yesterday afternoon I gave her two rupees before leaving home. "Why didn't you get kerosene?" I asked "I didn't find anyone," she retorted. She was looking for someone to go to the shop at the end of the street, the arrogant woman!'

'Your hands and legs couldn't have stayed still after that, could they?'

'If you don't get rice when you're hungry, what's the point of making money? I got very angry and slapped her four times!'

'You would have got your rice immediately! Has it not become a habit for you now to beat her every time she does something to annoy you?'

'You aren't going to understand, muthalali. Only when it actually happens to you will you understand the pain.'

'Did you go to bed hungry then?'

'I went to the food stall and picked up whatever was left over, and we both ate it. The whole house was leaking; I couldn't sleep a wink last night. She made some *uppuma*[28] for breakfast. I ate what she gave me and got ready to come here. Before I left, I casually asked her whether we had any rice, and she said no. I looked inside the rice bin and there wasn't a grain of rice. She had wiped it clean! How would you feel? When I asked why she had not told me about this yesterday, she said she just didn't! What do I do with her? Since I had beaten her up badly the previous night, her face was already swollen, so I

---

[28] A light meal made out of semolina

didn't have the heart to hit her again. Exasperated, I slapped my own head and came here!'

'Do you need to buy rice now so that she can start cooking?'

'What else? If I go to the fair price shop, there is a half-a-mile-long queue. Now, there is a rice shortage even in Thanjavur district, where paddy grows in abundance! Only when this government is ousted—'

'If your party comes to power, you will be going from house to house. If you talk politics now, you are going to go hungry. How much money do you want?' asked Kannan, handing him fifteen rupees. 'Don't stand in line at the fair price shop. Even if it is more expensive, buy rice from the general store.'

'I'll be back in half an hour,' said Saranathan as he left.

Kannan stepped out onto the street and looked up at the sky. While he could feel the heat of the sun, he could also see the clouds gathering. They were moving slowly, as if deep in thought and wondering when to strike again. 'It's going to be dangerous if it rains again today,' he mumbled as he went back inside the house. Hema was coming out just then. They crossed paths at the entrance. He moved aside to let her go while she, too, moved aside elegantly to make room for him to pass.

'I'll be back soon. Please don't forget me,' she said softly as he passed her.

He nodded silently and went inside. The sudden intimacy she demonstrated surprised him. Then, he remembered the rumours about her, which made him suspicious. If the rumours about her were true, he asked himself if she would be sympathetic towards Kausalai. Then, he began to fix the broken jari on the weft.

'How am I going to fix all this!' he sighed.

'It looks like half the jari is going to be wasted. It is all tangled up,' remarked Kausalai, entering the room.

'I'll fix it somehow or other, you'll see! What is Raji doing?'

'Sleeping.'

'She doesn't seem to know anything other than eating and sleeping.'

'The doctor has said it is going to be fine as time passes. Are they fighting constantly at Saranathan's house? He left as soon as he arrived!'

'He has gone to arrange for the next meal. If one person gives in, they wouldn't have these many fights. I have given in, so no fighting between us!'

'Yeah, right, you are really submissive, aren't you?' she said, pinching his thigh. 'Most people are distressed that they don't have money. When money comes looking for us, you're trying to find reasons to evade it.'

'Is this all your doing?' Kannan asked her.

'I didn't do anything. Hema told me that she is getting only a half per cent interest. She believes giving it to trustworthy people, like us, would be profitable for her. It's good for us also, isn't it? You don't have to be stunned. We aren't going to betray her. We'll divide the profits. We are always going to be paid for our work.'

'They are upper-class people. If her elder brother gets to know about it, we will be in big trouble. It could lead to unnecessary problems with people in high places. Just think about that.'

'We'll get money! That's the important thing. We'll keep clean accounts and act in good faith. What do we have to fear? If the elder brother finds out and asks us, we can always show him the accounts. Besides, she'll never tell her brother about this matter. And even if she does, it will only create problems for her.'

'For whatever reason...I feel afraid,' said Kannan, still hesitant.

Kausalai tried to convince him while trying to fix the jari: 'There is nothing to be afraid of. You hardly know Hema. She's a very good person and is quite fond of me. She will never do anything without my consent.'

'One cannot even trust one's own siblings these days. Whereas you!'

'Are all siblings going to be good? If we don't take her money, she's going to be very hurt.'

'Your wish. Why don't we seek your father's opinion as well?'

'Let's do that. He's not going to refuse any money that comes seeking us.'

## Chapter 16

It was past one thirty in the afternoon when Kannan finally sat down to eat. Kausalai had made *mochchai*[29] gravy with a lot of coconut pieces—not too spicy or sour. It tasted good.

'Do you have any coconut milk?' Kannan asked.

'I knew you were going to ask me that. There was only half a coconut, and I used it all up to make the gravy,' Kausalai responded.

Kannan liked to mix coconut milk with the rice and eat it with the lentil gravy. 'Imagine if I had responded like Saranathan to this response!'

'Would you have thrown the rice at me?'

'Kanna! Are you chatting with your wife? What concern do you have, with your rice bin full. All you have to do is keep

---

[29]Hyacinth beans

cooking. Only we know the trouble of getting some rice,' they heard a voice calling.

'Is that you Rangan?'

Kausalai peeked out to check. 'He hasn't come alone; there are few others with him,' she said.

'You are eating already?' asked Rangan as he entered the kitchen. 'We will probably get to eat our meal only around four or five this evening, but look at muthalali! He is enjoying freshly cooked samba rice at one o'clock,' he complained as he plopped down opposite Kannan.

Kannan smiled sympathetically, but Kausalai got angry. 'If he eats while you sit across and watch him, it is not going to sit well with him.' She said sharply to her husband, 'Get up! You can eat later!'

'Your woman is angry! What gravy is that? Won't you even invite your visitor to eat with you?' Rangan asked.

'The very sight of people eating is making you jealous, huh?' Kannan retorted.

'Kanna, you finish eating. Since there are a few others as well waiting for you, I'll wait outside. You can't afford to feed all of us!' said Rangan as he left the kitchen.

'We shouldn't let this fellow inside the house,' said Kausalai, frowning.

'Did I invite him? He should check before coming in,' Kannan said quietly, as he stuffed his mouth with buttermilk-rice, before springing to his feet.

Rangan was not alone; Balakrishnan, Suppian and

Kuppusamy were also waiting. Saranathan was seated behind them.

'Oh! You're all here in a group. What news?' Kannan inquired.

'Why would we come? Since we couldn't find any rice in this town, we came here to eat!' Kuppusamy responded.

'I'll gladly share my food. Am I going to be deprived of anything by feeding you?'

'Then we'll go home and bring our families with us. By then, the cooking can be done.'

'Food will be ready in half an hour.'

'Karnan[30] did go towards their backyard! This rich man, Kannan, has now started feeding the poor! We couldn't work in the rain, and when we ask the muthalali for money, he asks us, "Where will I go?" If we pawn our jari and yarn and go to the rice shop, we have to wait in line for three hours, and in the end, they give you half a kilo of some cheap variety of rice as if it is for charity. I sometimes seriously wonder if we are living in Kumbakonam or in the Sahara Desert. Congress came to power and the whole country has gone bankrupt. There is a shortage of everything except for babies and sickness!' blasted Balakrishnan, a communist sympathizer, who could not make up his mind whether he aligned with the Left or Right.

'Tell him why we have come to see him. We are here

---

[30]Karnan, one of the lead characters in the Indian epic Mahabharata, known primarily for his generosity towards everyone.

regarding union matters; don't mix politics with that. We're not going to do anything to undermine the government. We're only asking for rice. We are hungry; we will pay you, just give us some rice. That's all. What do we care about who the minister is? We're willing to work and are only asking for fair wages. We're also asking for rice at a fair price and to say anything beyond that would be wrong!' said Suppian.

Saranathan, who was seated at the very back, raised his voice a bit. 'It's because you've all been speaking so irresponsibly and feeding the bull[31] that it's behaving mulishly. We need to whip the bull into shape for it to respond!'

'The rising sun[32] has dissolved in the rain! Now, he has come to complain about the bull. Why indulge in all this unnecessary talk? Suppian is right. Workers and politics don't mix. What do you want me to do now?' asked Kannan.

'There's going to be a public meeting at the Birman Temple. Prices are rising by the day, and there is a shortage of rice. But if you're willing to pay a rupee per kilo, you can get any amount of rice. Shopkeepers are selling it openly, and what is the government doing about it? They are encouraging them and asking for their vote in return,' said Balakrishnan, harshly.

'Have you organized a meeting to condemn the government?' inquired Kannan.

---

[31] In those days, the symbol of the Congress Party was a pair of bulls carrying a yoke.
[32] The rising sun is the symbol of the Dravida Munnetra Kazhagam (DMK), a political party in Tamil Nadu.

'Balan is always like this. We are going to ask for a wage increase. You own your looms, will you join us?' asked Rangan.

'I, too, am a weaver. Does having two looms make me a muthalali? Whatever all of you decide to do, I'll join. At the current rate of inflation, it's only fair to demand higher wages.'

'You have to speak at the meeting. We're going to print your name on the notice.'

'Why? I'll speak but please don't publicize my name.'

'That is our prerogative. We just wanted to ask you. It's starting to drizzle; we need to leave before the rain starts.'

Everyone, except for Saranathan, left. 'It's getting close to Deepavali, and they are planning a strike now. Muthalalis usually give us fifty or hundred rupees, and now, we are going to lose that as well!' said Saranathan.

'Nothing like that is going to happen. Muthalalis will not allow that. Don't they know about inflation? If you ask for four, they will come down to at least one. What did you do all this while? Did you eat?' Kannan asked.

'With all this going on? I bought the rice and gave it to her. She just started cooking. I had some coffee at the food stall.'

## Chapter 17

The rain wreaked havoc on the weavers. Usually, silk weaving is not feasible during the rainy season. But, before Deepavali, when there is a high demand for silk, weavers place a clay pot of embers beneath the loom to keep the warp warm. Even then, weaving is not easy. Other than that, the rainy season means rest for weavers. They spend their time playing cards and board games and pursuing other activities of leisure. Womenfolk and children relax during this season as well.

But, this rainy season was not like any other. Even two-storey buildings were leaking and damp, let alone thatch- or tile-roofed houses. There was not a single dry spot in such houses. Silk and jari were valuable goods; just safeguarding them from the rain was hard enough. One or two members from each household went to rice and ration shops because it wasn't possible to buy everything in one shop. Besides, one had to ask around in multiple shops to get the best prices.

Rice, the staple, caused the biggest headache. With the ongoing shortages, finding rice was almost impossible. It was not possible to buy even two days' worth of rice. One could only buy enough rice for a day—sometimes just enough for a single meal. Rice was being sold at a rupee per unit, and even at that price, it was rationed at half a measure per person. The shopkeepers reasoned that the rice shortage was due to the rain, which was hindering them from drying the paddy. But no amount of logic could abate hunger!

Kannan did not face this problem, as he had saved enough rice stocks to last him a year. He had also stocked up on other basic provisions. So, unlike the other weavers, he did not have to run around searching for food supplies. Nevertheless, the rain tested him to the limit.

It rained from time to time, but when it did, the heavens opened, and it poured. Even though Kannan owned only a fifth of the house, it was boarded off from the rest, so he didn't have to encounter the others. He had electricity and tap water in the house and used the water from the well for dyeing the silk. He used the shared footpath adjoining the house just to access the toilet. But he realized that all these amenities were useless during the rains.

Even though the house was at a lower elevation than the street, there was a short, protective wall at the entrance of the house that blocked the street water from gushing in, but the rain decided to take an alternate route and attacked from the sky. He had bought an old house and had replaced the roof tiles a couple of times. Who knew how old the tiles were! Gradually, the rainwater started to seep through. The woven bamboo on the inner roofing had turned black with soot and cobwebs, and thus rainwater dripping from this surface turned everything pitch black, including the silk that it stained as it fell.

Kannan rolled up the warp and the jari and put them away, hoping to save them. But neither Kausalai nor he knew how to protect the rest of their belongings. Along the wall, there were stone storage troughs. But the damp was going to seep through the walls as well; soon, even the troughs began to collect water. What was to be done to save the paddy stored in the troughs?

Only the kitchen had escaped the deluge, as the glass roof tiles there had not dislodged to let the rainwater leak in. The floor was only slightly damp. Kannan and Kausalai hung the baby's hammock in the kitchen, spread gunny sacks on the floor under their sleeping mats and tried to sleep. Although Kannan was strong-willed, he was beginning to feel anxious. Despite her efforts to shore up his confidence, Kausalai was very uneasy. They could not fall asleep for a long time; they kept talking about the rain. Even crops and vegetation do not need so much rain, they said; there was news trickling in about the storm and the floods. *I'm only facing whatever everyone else is facing,* Kannan consoled himself, as he fell asleep.

How long had he slept? He awoke with a start when he heard something collapsing. First, he looked for the baby—was she safe? There was nothing going on in the kitchen. He came out holding a lamp. The wall in the main room had always had a big crack running across it. Now, about three feet of the wall had collapsed. He had woken up when the roof over that area had collapsed, causing the tiles to crash to the ground.

Kannan stood dumbstruck. He knew he could not do anything at that point. After standing there for a while, he went back to the kitchen quietly and woke up Kausalai.

'Kausalai! Wake up, the house has collapsed!'

'Whose house?' she asked as she sat up rubbing her eyes.

'Our house!'

'Our house? How can it collapse?'

'Come and see for yourself.'

As he retraced his steps with the lamp in his hand, she followed him. He wanted to confirm what he had seen.

'How terrible! How did it collapse?' she asked naively.

Kannan did not respond. How hard he had worked to own a home! Often, he had regretted getting a loan against it. Now, part of it had collapsed. What was he going to do? The silk and jari were damaged. Now the house was in danger as well. What was going to be his priority—his home or his livelihood? He couldn't attend to them both, but neglecting his livelihood meant facing certain hunger.

'What are we going to do if misfortune keeps piling upon us like this?' wept Kausalai on both their behalf.

'Adversity is to be overcome. Will weeping solve the problem? I'll stack those fallen roof tiles,' Kannan said as he walked towards the area where the wall and roof had collapsed.

'Please don't. The roof might collapse even more,' Kausalai pleaded.

'So, do you think we should wait until all the damage is done, huh? You're right, I suppose,' he said with an ironic laugh.

After that, both of them could not sleep. For a while, they kept checking to see whether the wall or the roof had suffered additional damage. Fortunately, things did not deteriorate any further. The remaining wall and roof stayed intact. The rain was streaming through the house and slowly draining away.

Kannan felt as if his mind had come to a standstill. He realized that continuing to talk about the damages and losses was going to further distress Kausalai. 'Now we have no option but to take Hema's money. I wonder if all this occurred so we would have to accept it. If all this has happened even before we take it, I wonder what's going to happen after?' Kannan reflected.

'You're talking through both sides of your mouth. Either way, you have to make up your mind and act upon it,' Kausalai reponded.

'You've decided, what am I going to say?'

She picked up the baby and began breastfeeding, and his thoughts were redirected.

*Since the baby was born, nothing has gone right*, thought Kannan. The baby was as beautiful as a ceramic doll but was also *like* a doll—inert. She cried only when she was hungry, and no one noticed her the rest of the time. She never smiled at anyone. They had seen all the doctors in town. Maybe they, too, could not understand the situation. 'Everything will be alright as time passes,' they said. Recently someone had advised him to go to Vellore[33] and consult the doctors there. *Adding losses upon losses—might as well do that*, he thought to himself.

The following morning, his friends crowded to see the collapsed wall and the roof. Kannan, too, better understood the damages then. Three feet of the wall had collapsed neatly; there was no danger to the rest of the wall. It would probably cost him five hundred rupees to get the wall and the roof fixed. But, if you planned for five hundred, in the current situation, it would probably cost seven hundred and fifty.

One of his two coconut trees in the backyard had been uprooted in the storm. Fortunately, the tree had not fallen on the house but towards the toilet area. Kannan and his neighbour, who owned the house behind his, did not get along well. If the tree had fallen over this neighbour's roof, he would have asked for damages. He was the kind of a person who would celebrate the damage to Kannan's house. When Kannan added up all the expenses and losses, he lost all confidence. Then, he started picking up the stones and the roof tiles, and a blind confidence sprung within him.

---

[33] A famous hospital in Vellore to which patients come from various parts of the country.

## Chapter 18

The weavers gathered at the Birman Temple for a public meeting. There are only a few temples for Brahma in India. The Kumbakonam deity is called Veda Narayana. Even though it is a small temple, it is beautiful in an understated way. This temple, along with the nearby Varatharaja Perumal temple, were administered by Saurashtrians. Earlier, social meetings used to take place at this temple, but now, such gatherings were rare.

Only on special occasions was the temple used for public meetings. Because of the heavy rain, the weavers were given permission to hold their meeting in the temple, where everyone could be accommodated comfortably. The rain, which had wreaked havoc, had suddenly vanished, and not a cloud was to be seen on the day of the meeting.

The president of the union, Subburao, who was not a weaver himself, presided over the meeting. He was not a party man either; he had worked for a couple of political parties and had left them. He was the president of many labour unions and understood the problems of workers first-hand. He was a full-time union leader. The weavers accepted his leadership because they believed that the silk industrialists would not be able to corrupt him.

Most of the weavers at the meeting were Saurashtrians; a few were Mudaliyars and some were Devanga Chettiars. Even though caste differences did not create any divisions among the weavers, party affiliations did. Many believed that caste distinctions created social ruptures in the country. But political differences even split families. In one family, the father might have been a Congressman, the elder son a Dravida Kazhagam member, the second son a communist and the third son a Dravida Munnetra Kazhagam cardholder. Every political party and ideology was represented among the weavers. When a party split and a new party was formed, there was room for that party as well. Just as politics was creating disorder in the country, it was doing the same to the weavers.

No matter which party one belonged to, everyone had a common problem. Prices were spiralling out of control. Therefore, the weavers' demanded for their wages to be raised by twenty-five per cent. This demand was formulated by the administrative committee of the union, believing that if you ask for twenty-five, you would end up with fifteen.

This demand was debated at the public meeting. Even though they had agreed not to bring politics into it, each speaker's analysis was from the perspective of his respective party. Communist sympathizer Balakrishnan was the first to speak: 'Our houses are floating in the flood; families are roaming around to find rice and lentils. If you ask muthalali for money, he firmly says "I can't give you anything extra." If you pawn your belongings and go to the shop, they tell you "No rice." When they tell you to eat wheat instead, we look for wheat and can't find that either. We tried eating ragi, but our ungrateful stomachs are rebelling. What is this government, which sheds crocodile tears under the pretext of ruling on behalf of the poor, doing about it? What are the capitalists who carry the palanquins of the rulers doing? This capitalist rule—'

Before Balakrishnan could continue, the president interrupted: 'Just speak about why we are here. We shouldn't dwell on unrelated topics.'

'I'm *not* talking about unrelated matters.'

'If we allow for political talk, this meeting will never end.'

'I can't speak according to your wishes; I'll speak the way I want. Let good speakers continue,' Balakrishnan said angrily and went back to his seat.

Next, it was Saranathan's turn. The previous night his lymph nodes had swollen, and he had had a bout of fever. Since these flare-ups had become a regular occurrence every two to three months, he usually had the medication ready. He took his medication, and when the fever subsided, attended the meeting. He did not like the fact that the president had interrupted Balakrishnan's speech. He belonged to a radical group that worked for progress and opened his speech dramatically.

'In October, a unit of rice was sixty-five paise; in November it was a hundred and twenty-five. In October, a kilo of dried chilies was three rupees; in November, it was eight. In October, a unit of salt was four paise; in November, that too doubled. You weave all day long, and before you can get ten rupees out of the muthalali, tears of blood begin streaming from your eyes. If you go to the shop with ten rupees, you can't even get something worth its weight. Who can you blame? If you blame the politicians, our president says don't talk politics. If we say to our muthalais, "with rising prices and stagnant wages, can't you give us a raise?", the president would stop us by saying "don't rebuke the muthalalis". Then who do we blame? The only right left to us weavers is to break our wives' backs. Sheesh! What an awful life it is for us weavers!' concluded Saranathan and quickly got off the stage. The resounding cheer that followed made it seem as if the temple would collapse.

A murmur rippled through the crowd. Ramamurthy stepped onto the stage. He was a Dravida Kazhagam volunteer, and his face was flushed listening to Saranathan's speech. He began his speech furiously: 'Blaming the government for everything has become a habit for us. Are we obeying the government? When the government keeps begging us to not have too many children, do we listen? We continue to have a child every year. Agricultural output is growing, but it is unable to keep pace with the growing population. In this situation, how can the cost of living come down? True-blooded Tamils are ruling Tamil Nadu, and the whole world is praising their rule. Those who criticize our government are traitors. It's a Brahmin plot—'

The president banged on the table, interrupting Ramamurthy: 'We are asking for a wage increase. Please provide your arguments about that. *That* should suffice.'

Ramamurthy held on to the microphone and shouted: 'I didn't say not to raise the wages! How can you allow the authentic Tamil rule to be criticized? I will not get off the stage without responding.'

The president was a sly fox. 'Alright, please step down. Kannan will speak next,' he said firmly.

The president was a strict man, so Ramamurthy did not want to linger any longer; he also knew that he didn't have much support from the audience. So, he said, 'I condemn the president for being biased,' and left the stage.

It was Kannan's turn next. The president knew that Kannan was a good speaker and would stick to the point, and therefore asked him to speak last. Kannan was very disturbed by all the disastrous things that had happened to him over the past few days. Since he knew that he was going to be invited to speak, he had carefully listened to what the others had to say. When the president called his name, he was both resolute and calm as he reached the podium.

'The prices keep going up; we didn't gather here to debate who is responsible. Our only demand is that wages must keep pace with inflation. We call silk manufacturers muthalalis, but they are not millionaires, like Tata and Birla. If this rain continues for a few more days not only the weavers but half the muthalalis, too, will be devastated. We aren't mill workers. Every morning, the first thing we have to face is our muthalalis. If we destroy them, we, too, will be ruined in the process. This is our reality. If the weavers and muthalalis make enemies of each other, neither group will survive. Both sides must accommodate each other; that is beneficial for both.

'The muthalalis are quite aware of the input prices rising like poison. It's futile to expect them to raise our wages without us asking. The administrative committee has decided to ask for a quarter rupee raise per rupee. All of you should accept that demand wholeheartedly.

'Let's convey our decision to the muthalalis; I believe that they will accept our demand. Our muthalalis are compassionate and broad-minded—they understand our problems. They'll definitely accept our demand. Deepavali is barely a month away, and the business is brisk. At this time, they are not going to risk a strike. Therefore, let's all hope that things will be settled amicably,' Kannan said.

The president did not call on anyone else after that. 'We'll inform the manufacturers of our demand through leaflets and give them a fifteen-day grace period. If they don't respond to our demand within that period, we can begin our strike. If we are forced to go on a strike, at that time, let's have another public meeting,' he concluded.

The decision was accepted unanimously.

When Kannan returned home after the meeting, it was

well past ten. He hadn't had any direct contact with the manufacturers for some time now. The weavers who were in direct contact with them believed that the muthalalis would not agree to a wage increase. The muthalalis' argument was, 'In places like Kanchipuram and Thanjavur, the wages are not any higher, then why should we raise wages here?' In this situation, if the weavers began a strike, how long would they be able to sustain it? They had already missed a lot of work due to the rain. If they began a strike in this weakened condition, Kannan believed that they would not be able to survive it.

What bothered Kannan and the others was that whenever the price of silk or jari went up, the muthalalis immediately raised the prices of the saris they sold, so why don't they have the heart to raise the weavers' wages and increase the sari prices? *Money kills humanity; this is true not only of individuals but also societies,* Kannan reflected. 'Even if they don't accept our entire demand, we will come to a good end,' Kannan had expressed hopefully to his friends before he left.

When he reached home, Kausalai was waiting for him on the front porch. 'Can't you come home as soon as the meeting is over? My father has taken ill. A messenger was sent to inform us. Come and eat,' she said with concern.

*What has happened to my father-in-law?* Kannan wondered. Yes, Kausalai's father was old. It has been five years since his sixtieth birthday. Yet, no one would guess he was a day over fifty. He was the only one who cared for his son-in-law's well-being. Kannan and Kausalai had been planning to seek his advice regarding the damages they had suffered. What must have happened for Kausalai's family to send someone to inform them?

'He went to bed with a fever last night. He hadn't taken any medication. Since early morning, he has been drifting in and out of consciousness and then he asked to see you and me,' Kausalai shared.

'Oh Rama!'

## Chapter 19

Kannan's father-in-law had passed away by the time they reached his house. Those who had been by his deathbed said that he had been murmuring about Kannan and Kausalai until the end. Being his only daughter, Kausalai was very attached to her father. When she heard the news, she beat her head and chest and began wailing at the top of her voice, so much so that she lost her voice after the funeral! She didn't even realize that her baby had slipped from her hips. Four women had to hold her down to stop her from hurting herself.

Lamenting at funerals is a special art. Professional women mourners had already gathered at Kausalai's family home and were lamenting with rhyme and rhythm. Even though Kausalai was quite new to it, she joined them, and soon became quite adept. After she found this vent for her grief, her frenzy subsided.

Whether it is a wedding or a funeral, the son-in-law

always plays a prominent role. Since Kannan was his late father-in-law's only son-in-law, he had many responsibilities and duties at the funeral. For Kannan, his father-in-law had been a pillar of strength, and Kannan had depended on him to solve problems and for support. Kannan was shocked by his sudden demise. Kausalai's wailing and frenzy influenced him. Genuine grief is not sophisticated. He, too, fell to the ground and began rolling and crying. The funeral-goers had the task of consoling him. How long can one weep? They had to perform the final rites and cremate the body. Kannan had to take the lead in these matters. So, he controlled himself and took care of his duties.

It was a big loss for the family, and they displayed it by bidding Kausalai's father a grand farewell. They served light snacks for the attendees. When they lit firecrackers, it was like a celebration for the grandchildren. Some adults also joined in the merriment. Musicians followed the funeral procession singing religious hymns.

Customarily, funeral expenses are shared among close relatives in fixed ratios. Sons-in-law are expected to bear the biggest burden. Kannan was the only son-in-law, and therefore he had to provide the food for the funeral house for the first two days. He was also expected to provide new clothes for his brothers-in-law for the thirteenth-day ceremony: the day was also marked by a special meal. Fortunately, his mother-in-law had already passed away, or else, he would have had to give her a silk sari. One could not economize on any of these expenses.

When Kannan realized his share of the expenses was going to be around two hundred rupees, his misery deepened.

His father-in-law's death was a big loss for Kannan. If only he had been alive and lucid when they had arrived at his deathbed, he would have definitely given his daughter something. There was gossip that the night before his father-in-law had been quite lucid and had advised his sons to divide up everything amicably and to give Kausalai a thousand rupees. Even amidst her weeping, this information reached Kausalai's ears, and she pulled Kannan aside and informed him. But, neither Kannan nor Kausalai expected her brothers to follow through on their father's wish. They did not raise this issue during the first couple of days. Kausalai decided to broach this topic after all the funeral commotion was over.

On the first day, they cremated the body; on the second day, they sprinkled the ashes in the river; and on the third day, Kannan and Kausalai returned to their own house. As the daughter of the house, Kausalai was duty-bound to stay at their father's house. But, she and Kannan had left their house in a hurry. The collapsed wall and the roof of their house had not been secured, and therefore both of them wanted to return and check on the house.

There was another surprise waiting for Kausalai. Her baby, who had never cried and laughed, had started saying 'mmm-maa-maa!' It looked like she was expressing some emotions. When the baby saw her mother crying, she started crying too. How beautiful she looked, even when she cried.

However, Kausalai could not appreciate the child's responses at the funeral. Both Kannan and Kausalai were curious to see if their daughter's emotional development continued after returning home.

With all that crying, Kausalai's face was swollen and she had almost lost her voice. She was the very definition of how a daughter should properly grieve her lost father. This grief was compounded by the concern about the damage to their house and looms. As soon as they reached home, she and Kannan crowded around Raji.

'Darling Raji! Say Amma!' begged Kausalai.

'Mmm-maa-maa!' babbled Raji, reaching for her mother.

When their baby, who had seemed not only deaf and dumb but also unresponsive, began to babble, the parents were overjoyed. They forgot their own problems and spent a long time playing with her. Kausalai invited a couple of her neighbours to see this wonder.

'I think she waited until my father passed away for me to cry!' she said as she wove her sadness into her happiness.

'Your uncontrollable weeping must have shocked the baby!' Kannan said.

'What about you—rolling on the floor like women and weeping!' Kausalai retorted.

'I just couldn't bear it. He was here just ten days ago; he left so suddenly!'

'It was our bad luck that he passed away before we could see him. It's apparently true that he wanted to give me a thousand rupees. I'm not going to let go. I'm going to ask—'

'They'll not give you anything. With your father's passing, our connection to that household is also gone. If you ask for money, there's going to be unnecessary hard feelings.'

'If there's going to be a misunderstanding, so be it. At least I will get to know what kind of people my siblings are!'

'Get to know them!' laughed Kannan. 'They're already talking about how to divide everything up. It seems like there is going to be a fight among the brothers. You can go and shout in the middle of everything, but before that, make sure you get your voice back. Even I can hardly hear you!'

## Chapter 20

It was not even ten in the morning when the shop boy from Chakrapani Iyer's jari store arrived. Kannan owed four hundred rupees to the shop owner, and Chakrapani was the kind of person who did not even trust the veshti around his waist. Kannan had been able to get supplies on loan only because of his father-in-law's recommendation. Chakrapani must have heard about the losses and expenses that Kannan had suffered recently. In addition, his patron, the father-in-law, was also no more!

Kannan returned with the shop boy to the jari store. On his way to the store, he pondered over the response he would give Chakrapani. Kannan did not intend to default on any of his loans. He decided to ask Chakrapani for two or three additional months to settle the loan. He explained everything that had happened in detail.

Chakrapani listened to everything Kannan had to say with

a smile on his face. 'What's the urgency in returning the loan? First, sort out your problems. I didn't call you because of that. I need a sari for Deepavali and heard you are going on a strike. Will I get one?'

Kannan understood that Chakrapani was cunningly trying to get the loan repaid in kind instead of cash, and even if he inflated the price by ten or twenty rupees, Chakrapani would agree to it. All said and done, he had to settle the loan, and this way, he could make some additional profit.

'To rebuild the weaving platform and begin work, it'll take at least a week. If the strike begins after that, I can't do anything. If we are not on strike, I'll definitely weave a sari for you. Is one enough? Even if you want two, you can have them. I don't have any in light colours; only blue and black.'

'One for my wife and one for my daughter—give me two, with border and contrasting thread work in the body, alright?'

'Of course.'

'For the quality of the jari, light colours will not be attractive. It will be good if you can give them to me for Deepavali. If not, give them to me afterwards. It's not as if they have to be worn on that day,' said Chakrapani.

'I'll definitely get it to you. As long as my debt is settled, I am fine!'

'The debt is no big deal! Give me the saris and take whatever jari you need!' Chakrapani concluded.

Kannan bade him goodbye and stood up. From his conversation, Kannan understood that after receiving his two saris, Chakrapani would not be giving Kannan any jari on loan in the future. Once he gave Chakrapani his two saris, his loan would be paid off. Chakrapani had loaned him supplies based on trust and had never been stern with him; and, in return, he had never exhibited any untrustworthy behaviour. Given all this, why had Chakrapani lost faith in him all of a sudden? Maybe Chakrapani had heard about all the losses he had suffered? Was it because his father-in-law was no more?

*Does he not trust me at all? Only when he has a house, jewellery and so on does a man command respect; there is no respect for the man himself! Chakrapani wants his loan to be repaid, and I will do just that,* Kannan comforted himself.

Right by the jari store was the Kora silk store. He owed about two thousand rupees to them. Kannan thought it would be best to pay a visit there before someone was sent to fetch him. Murari Jayaramiyer's family had been in the silk trade for generations. Once upon a time, they had even imported silk from China and Japan. In silk manufacturing, one has to loan materials, and all of it is done on the basis of trust. Jayaramiyer was the incarnation of trust; he would not trust anyone easily, but once he did, it was well known that he would not hesitate to loan thousands of rupees worth of supplies to a person. Kannan knew this through his own experience. His father-in-law had initially introduced him to Jayaramiyer and recommended him for a loan of five hundred rupees. But, within a mere three months, Jayaramiyer had loaned him over two thousand rupees worth of supplies. He trusted Kannan and wanted him to succeed. Kannan felt that it was his duty to let him know what had happened to him.

Jayaramiyer welcomed him warmly. When Kannan saw him, grey-haired, with holy ash smeared on his broad forehead, his confidence resurged.

'Come in, Kanna, sit down!' he said. As soon as Kannan sat down, Jayaramiyer began speaking: 'I heard everything. The wall collapsed and the loom was damaged? Your father-in-law need not have left in such a hurry. If he had been here, he would have been a great support to you.'

'I actually came here to convey all this to you. You have to be a little patient with me; you loaned me money based on trust, and I'll never let you down,' said Kannan in a humble voice.

'Without trust, how can one be in this business? Don't worry about the balance owed to me. I know you want to return the loan and that I'll eventually get paid. You sort out your problems. You can repay me in instalments of two or three hundred rupees at a time as and when you get money. If you give me two hundred rupees, I'll give you yarn worth that amount. If we do it on a rolling basis, I'll also be satisfied with the arrangement. Is that alright?'

Kannan liked this arrangement very much. Jayaramiyer did not even ask Kannan to reduce the balance owed to him, in stark contrast with the jari store owner.

'Listen carefully to what I have to say. You should not believe everything you see, but you need trust to be in this business. Before trusting someone, you need to think deeply about that relationship. Saranathan came here yesterday,' Jayaramiyer said.

'But I didn't send him!' Kannan responded, surprised.

'He wants to get his own loom. He asked me to lend him supplies. There's nothing wrong with that; everyone likes to start their own business. He advised me to get your loan repaid soon, since you're finding it difficult to raise your head again; you have to repair your house and fix your two looms, and nothing seems to be going well for you recently. He also mentioned that your wife was wearing a ten- or twelve-sovereign gold chain around her neck! He told me to ask you for that.'

This was shocking news—Saranathan had done this! For many years they had been like brothers. How did he get this terrible idea all of a sudden? They had not even had a small misunderstanding!

'I'm really surprised by what you have just told me! I can't believe that he would do something like this!'

'Every man has both good and bad within him. I am not saying Saranathan is a bad fellow. He thinks that I will trust him only if he presents himself as protecting my financial interests. Let bygones be bygones, but in the future, be cautious. Only a man who can figure out how much trust to place on outsiders will succeed in life. Don't torment yourself over the losses you have suffered. Go! Work confidently.'

When Jayaramiyer said this, as if bidding him goodbye, Kannan stood up.

## Chapter 21

When his father-in-law passed away, Kannan felt as if he had lost one hand. Now, it felt as if Saranathan had broken his other hand. He had trusted Saranathan so much! Had Saranathan put on an act all these days? One treacherous act kindled many suspicions in Kannan now. Saranathan had taken care of all his accounts. When he went to Tirupati, his budget had swollen like an ocean. The losses that year had ended up being much more than what Kannan had expected! Saranathan blamed the muthalali for it. Now Kannan began to suspect that Saranathan might have been dishonest in his dealings. Kannan could not doubt him entirely either. He acted like a family member; why this pettiness all of a sudden? Maybe he believed that Kannan would not be able to emerge from his many debts? Or was he planning to undermine Kannan now?

Kannan had no doubt that Saranathan would have

bad-mouthed him at the jari store, just like he had done at the silk store. The silk shop owner was a good person and had been very accommodating. If Jayaramiyer had also tried to drag Kannan down like the jari shop owner, what would his plight have been? He would definitely have gone under.

'I just can't believe it. Even though we are from different castes, we have associated with him like family! How did he have the heart to do this to us?' said Kausalai.

'He has the heart alright! I'm so angry! Shall I go drag him here?' Kannan asked, still reeling from the shock.

'Don't do that. He will come on his own. What are you going to achieve by getting angry? We should end our relationship with him,' said Kausalai. She was not the kind of person who went out looking for a fight. But, at the same time, she was also not one to let go of a fight when it came her way. Her throat was still sore from her grief-stricken wailing at the funeral, and she could barely speak. Maybe that was why she was avoiding a fight now!

'What's left for us in this relationship to end? Has he not broken it off himself?'

'Let him go! Let him be well and leave us alone.'

'This is good. At least we finally got to know him.'

'Now stop this talk. When he comes, don't say anything to show him that you know what he has done to us. Let's see what he has to say. Once he has had his last word, we can say there is nothing left between us and go our separate ways. Until then, why not fix those glass roof tiles?' Kausalai suggested.

For two days, there had been no sign of any rain. 'In October if it rains it rains, and if it shines it burns,' was a common saying that seemed to be coming true. The heat after the rains was intense. The roof tiles were completely dry. So, now, there was no danger of them breaking under Kannan's weight. He climbed on top of the roof and rearranged the dislodged tiles. He tied them with ropes so that they would not budge again in rain or wind.

The roof had collapsed over Saranathan's loom platform. Only after repairing the wall and the roof could Saranathan weave again. Maybe he had decided to part ways because of that! Kannan's weaving platform had also dissolved in the rain. Kannan stacked up bricks, mixed the mud into a paste and began repairing his platform.

It was then that Saranathan turned up at their house. In the meantime, Kannan's mental anguish had subsided to a great extent. He decided that Kausalai's conclusion of cutting loose from Saranathan was the best path forward.

'Are you done with your father-in-law's funeral duties? Expenses keep piling up!' Saranathan said. Although he was conveying his condolences, his voice seemed very lively; the thought of having his own looms had probably put him in high spirits! Kannan was not worried about the expenses. But he *was* surprised at how enthusiastic Saranathan seemed while backstabbing him; but Kannan did not permit any of these emotions to show.

'We've to be prepared for everything, right? Can one be afraid of expenses? Can you live under the sky and be afraid of lighting?'

'I didn't mean it that way. What I meant was that if your father-in-law had been alive, he would've been of great support to you at this juncture. I feel sad about his demise.'

Kannan reminded himself that Saranathan could be deceitful. But, he could sense grief in Saranathan's voice!

'Any news of a strike? I've no idea what has happened in the past few days,' Kannan inquired.

'What's going to happen? They have given notice. Muthalalis are going to negotiate with our president. What do you think that will lead to? They'll probably agree to give us one or two rupees more per sari!' Saranathan responded.

'Are we going to get everything we ask for? First we should accept whatever they agree to give and then continue our struggle.'

Saranathan laughed out loud: 'Aren't you a small muthalali? What else would you say?'

'You, too, are going to be a muthalali soon,' said Kannan at this opportune moment.

When he heard this, Saranathan was dumbfounded; he started suspecting that Kannan must have visited the jari shop.

'Where would I find the energy for that? If there was peace in my household, I could've had ten looms. One brother dumped his money on a cow and is now struggling; another one is saying that this vocation is beneath him. Where do I have the money to have my own loom?'

'Why do you need your own capital to have your own loom? If you get the silk and jari on loan, the loom becomes yours!' said Kannan.

Saranathan's doubts were cleared now. He understood that either the jari shop owner or the silk shop owner had told Kannan the truth. He thought, *nobody is going to trust me and loan anything. I am also not going to have my own loom!*

Kausalai had been listening to everything. Although she had pacified Kannan earlier, she could not hold back another minute. She burst out and started cursing him in a hoarse voice, 'Go ahead and get your own loom! Live well! Are we stopping you? Why do you feel that you have to ruin someone else's life in order for you to have a good life? You have been bad-mouthing us at the jari and silk store! How is that fair? Have we ever done you a bad turn? Being treacherous after associating like brothers all these years—do you think you will do well in life?'

Saranathan's face revealed his embarrassment. Yet, he pretended to be angry and blustered: 'We men are having a conversation. Why are you getting involved? Once words are spilled, they cannot be taken back. Speak calmly! Who told you that I had spoken about you at the jari and silk shop?'

Kannan was losing his patience. 'The silk shop owner, Jayaramiyer, has had his doubts about you for a long time! He is the one who told me.'

Saranathan calmed down but was not ready to accept that he had lied. 'So he told you? I can't believe it. It has been more than a month since I saw him.'

Even though Kannan was angry, he kept his head cool: 'Then are you saying that I am lying? Look here, Saranatha! We have been like family. Once, you even pawned your wife's jewellery to loan me money. I have always been fair to you. If we fight like this, others are going to laugh at us. Let's settle our accounts today itself.'

'I've always known that you would do something like this. Can't you bid me well and send me off? Why are you slandering me before parting ways? Did I ever behave like an outsider with you? I pawned our jewellery and gave you money; wasn't it me who prepared all your statements for income taxes? Have you forgotten everything I did for you?'

'Yes, and *we* have not done anything for you in return! You have been very loyal,' Kausalai interrupted.

'Why all this unnecessary talk? You don't need me anymore. You know you'll have to give me fifty or a hundred rupees for Deepavali, so you have decided to send me away now and save that money. Alright, go ahead!'

When Kannan saw that Saranathan had not only dug a hole for him to fall in but was now also trying to push him down, he burst out angrily: 'Saranatha, leave respectfully! Not only have you been dishonest in your dealings, but you are now being arrogant too!'

'I'm not going to be waiting around here. If you finalize the account and give me what's mine—'

'What accounts? You already have an extra hundred and fifty rupees!'

'Don't you still have to pay me for maintaining the accounts? Is that free for you?'

'Even if we take out fifty for the accounting work you've done, isn't it you who still owes me a hundred rupees? Have you forgotten that too? You don't have to return that hundred. Just don't step into this house again!'

'By repeatedly stepping into this house, I have become Kuberan[34]. Isn't that enough?' Saranathan said stiffly and left.

'I trusted people who were close to me and they, in turn, stabbed me in the back—it's my stupidity!' Kannan said as Saranathan left.

'Do you think he's going to keep quiet? He seems like a very cunning fellow!' said Kausalai, revealing her anxiety.

'What's he going to do? He'll go to the jari store and exaggerate everything. He has no place in the silk store. He'll probably go to the place where I have got the loan on our house and gossip about me. Let him! We can't live in fear. I have my measuring tape and am good at what I do. What can anyone do to us?'

Kausalai felt proud to hear this. She handed the baby over

---

[34]Kuberan is considered the treasurer of the gods and portrayed as being wealthy. Here Saranathan is being sarcastic, as he is very poor.

to Kannan and said, 'Now that she has learned a word, she doesn't stop calling me!'

'Is she calling only for her mother? What about her father?' asked Kannan as he lifted the baby up and kissed her.

## Chapter 22

Kannan felt as if he had lost everything. He had scolded Saranathan and chased him away, and now, felt remorseful about it. Does anger *ever* come out in a measured way? But then how could he not get angry? This world is full of good and bad people, and we have to trust others in order to survive. Even thieves have a truth within themselves. It is only among those of us who pretend to be good people that the truth is slowly withering away. Who should Kannan trust? His siblings had chased him out with only the clothes on his back! While his mother's body had still been at home, they had fought over the gold chain around his mother's neck—accursed people!

Saranathan had behaved like a brother with Kannan. He had practically lived with Kannan and learned his strengths and weaknesses. Had he been waiting for an opportunity to stab Kannan in the back? That cannot be! He took advantage of

Kannan's weakness to help himself! You can fight your enemy, as he does not know your limitations, but you cannot battle with a friend, as he knows all your weaknesses. After all, we have revealed to him where our weak spots are! If a muthalali cheats a worker, one can understand; but a worker ruining another worker? Maybe he had started calling Kannan muthalali because he felt he could not cheat another worker!

The only person who had genuinely wanted to help Kannan had been his father-in-law, and he had departed without even bidding farewell. Kannan had four brothers-in-law, but they were in such a hurry to divide up their father's estate. In this situation, were they going to even consider being fair to their sister?

They were not the kind of people to be considerate towards others. It had been five days since his father-in-law passed away. Every day there was turmoil in that household. Each person was grabbing whatever he could lay his hands on. In a household that had been full of copper and brass utensils, one could not even find a cup to drink water—all the kitchen utensils had disappeared! Replaced by aluminium and ceramic utensils. Each one of them was pretending to be a saint yet did not know where all the household goods had vanished! In this situation, how could one expect them to honour their father's wish and give Kausalai a thousand rupees? In the past five days, they had not even mentioned that such a conversation had taken place before he died!

Kannan was not expecting that money. But, now, he badly

needed some money. First, he had to get his house repaired. If he did not get the wall fixed, it was going to degrade, and they would lose all security and shelter. In one way or another, he had to find some money. If Kausalai's jewellery was pawned, they might be able to get five hundred rupees. But, given the circumstances, she would have to go to her family's house often. How could she appear without anything on her neck? What of her respectability? So, this was not a good time to pawn her jewellery. He had a thousand rupees worth of silk and jari in stock, but he did not have the heart to dip into his capital. Since morning he had been roaming around to secure some money and was able to come up with only a hundred rupees. It was not even sufficient to cover his share of the funeral expenses! With no other option, he decided to pawn the silk and jari.

Kausalai had finished cooking and was getting ready to go to her parents' house. It was customary for her to stay at the funeral home until the thirteenth day after the funeral. Since there was no other help in her own house, she was going between the two houses. She cooked daily at her house, and then went over to her parents' house. Each night, after lighting the lamp, female relatives lamented and wailed. Once that was over, she returned home. By the time Kannan got home, she was back and waiting for him to return.

'Don't worry about anything. Why do we have my jewellery if not to help us through hardship? You can pawn the silk and the jari for now, and once my father's rituals are over, we can pawn my jewellery and redeem the silk and the jari,' said

Kausalai, agreeing with Kannan's plans. Her voice was beginning to return, and she spoke confidently.

'I, too, have come to the same conclusion. I'll have the money ready today or tomorrow. I asked the mason to come the day after tomorrow. If Saranathan finds out about us pawning the silk and jari, do you know what he'll be up to?'

'He will gossip all over town. That is why God himself has separated him from us! Why bother about him? We need to take care of ourselves.'

'I can't stop thinking about how closely we associated with him!'

'Stop talking about that. We don't have anyone who cares about us anymore. We should not be disgraced in the eyes of others. We should somehow or other survive and retain our respectability. After we are done with my father's duties, we can meet Hema.'

'Have you not seen her at all?'

'She came in the morning, but you had gone out. She is very firm about her decision. She has already asked the moneylender to return her money. I told her that we could finalize everything after my father's ceremonies are over. God will never let us down. You'll see that we will not lack for anything.'

'I can see that. The baby that was mute all these days is calling you.'

'What's the next baby going to be?' laughed Kausalai.

'If it's going to be a girl, I'm not going to speak to you.'

'Just for saying that I'm going to have a baby girl, you'll see!'

## Chapter 23

Kannan felt confident with Kausalai by his side. However, as soon as she left, worries enveloped him. Kausalai was belligerent but not without a good reason. When she saw that something was unfair, she did not let it pass. He was afraid that she might end up in a big fight with her brothers. Even if his brothers-in-law refused to give them the money, at least they would have relatives to associate with! He could not stop thinking about his father-in-law, who had visited him only fifteen days back. He had wanted Kannan's life to be free of the burden of debt. He had also wanted Kannan to own five or six looms and live well. He had even promised to do his best to help Kannan. What was the point of thinking of all that now?

Everything dear to him was beginning to slip away. He was enjoying living in his own home, but now, its debt burden was compounded by damage. He had always wanted his own looms, and now, he was on the verge of losing them as well. Kausalai's jewellery would be useful, but he had to make sure that he would be able to redeem it.

He had not felt this weary even when he had been destitute, not knowing where his next meal would come from. Long after Kausalai had left for her family house, he ate his dinner for the sake of eating, lay down and fell into an exhausted slumber.

He had not locked the door. Usually, even the smallest sound used to wake him up. So, the sound of the creaking front door as someone entered the house startled him awake. He got up quickly and was taken aback when he saw Hema closing the door behind her. So accustomed to being deferential toward rich people, his body bowed automatically and respectfully.

'Come in,' he said, trying to convey that Kausalai was not home.

'Has Kausalai gone to her mother's house?' Hema asked.

'Yes, she cooked dinner and left. She'll return tonight but I can't say what time she will be back,' said Kannan. He expected her to leave when she heard this.

When she spoke next, her voice was more respectful than Kannan's tone towards her. It was something one never heard in a wife's voice.

'It's a pity, as you never expect an elder to pass away like this. It's as if lightning has struck Kausalai. If I so much as mention her father, she starts crying.'

This did not seem like the end of a conversation—more like the beginning of one. Kannan stood silent.

'It's like you lost one of your hands, right?' Hema inquired.
'Yes,' Kannan responded.
'What do you plan to do now?'
'What are you talking about?'
'What we had talked about.'
'Neenga—'
'I'm much younger than you yet you address me so respectfully as if I am an old woman! I feel very awkward when you speak to me like this!'
'Should I be respectful based on age?'
'You don't have to be respectful for any reason. Just be affectionate. That is enough. I don't think of you and I as separate. You still think of me as an outsider?'

Kannan now remembered Kausalai mentioning Hema's visit in the morning when he had not been home. He realized that Hema was there, then, knowing full well that Kausalai was not home, which made him suspicious and worried. Four families lived in the house. If anyone were to see them together, it would lead to vicious gossip. Should she not be more afraid than him about gossip? She did not seem to be worried at all.

'Why are you just standing there speechless?' Hema demanded of Kannan.
'Nothing. Kausalai has her opinion on this matter.'
'You don't?'
'It's not that I don't have one. Let's decide when Kausalai is here.'
'Kausalai agreed to it a long time back. I have asked for

the money and should have it in a week or so. I'll give it to you when I get it.'

'Why don't you sit and talk?'

'When you're standing, how can I sit?'

He sat down after giving her a box of betel leaves.[35] It was as if he finally understood the real reason why she was there; he was still afraid to believe it.

'I don't chew betel leaves,' she said and took the box from him and sat down cosily. She took out four betel leaves and prepared them for chewing by adding areca nut and lime, and then neatly folding them. She got up and politely gave it to him and said, 'Here.'

Kannan felt sheepish but understood the situation. He still felt afraid. 'You...what is this?' he asked as he took the betel leaves and put them in his mouth. Stiffness came over his body! He could not think of anything other than the fact that he had Hema's betel preparation in his mouth.

'Shouldn't I give it to you? Is it not good?' Hema responded coyly.

'If you talk like this—'

'You keep talking to me so courteously! I'll tell you what is on my mind without hiding anything,' she said, her voice choking. She did not continue speaking. She took off her diamond earrings, necklace and six pairs of bangles. As Kannan did not understand why she was taking them off, he silently

---

[35]The offering and acceptance of betel leaves signifies intimacy and loyalty.

watched her. Hema was physically smaller than Kausalai and more youthful.

'Will you never believe me? Why do I need all this—you keep it!' she said as she stuffed her jewellery into his hands.

Since Kannan was emotionally overwhelmed, he sat there, dazed. He saw her standing there as if she did not have anything to hide. He was not oblivious to the fact that the one who had declared that she had no needs, in fact, needed much. She did not say anything; he could not say anything. Both of them were well-versed connoisseurs—they savoured each other in perfect harmony.

## Chapter 24

Hema felt like just lying there! But when Kannan heard the bullock cart halting at the entrance, his heart was in his mouth.

'Kausalai has arrived!' he said, jumping up.

'Oh my God!'

'Hmm...quick!' he hurried her. In the rush, she did not know what to do and what not to do as she dashed to the door.

'You've forgotten your jewellery!' he said as he stuffed them into the pallu of her sari; she held on to the pallu and the jewellery and ran towards the front entrance; she opened the front door and had not even taken four steps when Kausalai appeared!

Hema was terrified and could not find any words for a few seconds: 'I came to see you. He said you were not home yet. I was just leaving,' she muttered.

Kausalai did not say anything. She understood what had

happened when she saw Hema's hair and sari in disarray. Does a wife not know how her husband likes to play? When she realized that her treasure had been looted, she was furious.

'Have you been here for a long time?' she interrogated Hema like a criminal.

'I just arrived, and when I found out you were not home, I was leaving.'

'Didn't you tell me that you were going to come tomorrow morning? Did you come looking for me just when you knew I wouldn't be here?'

Hema realized that Kausalai had understood what had happened; she wanted to get out at any cost, but how to get past Kausalai?

'What are you saying, Kausalai? How can you speak like this?' she said in a subdued voice.

'I understand everything! Is this why you wanted to help us?'

'Speak softly. Why are you shouting?'

'Why should *I* speak softly; did I steal like you? What's that in your pallu?' Kausalai did not stop at that; she grabbed and yanked Hema's pallu. Hema had not had the time to tie the jewellery into a bundle and so it scattered all over the floor; the bangles rolled away.

Hema got distracted by the scattered jewellery. She squatted down and started picking it up.

'Oh, this too, huh? So, are you ensnaring him by giving him your jewellery now? If you give money in the hands of a widow and let her run around town, what else can you expect?'

Kausalai was spewing vitriol faster than time itself. Kannan stood by the door, tortured, not knowing when to intervene. He felt afraid that his neighbours might appear. He was also terrified that someone might be watching this drama. 'Why talk in the street? Come inside!' he said.

'Of course, where else am I going?'

The baby, who had been fast asleep on Kausalai's hips, woke up and began crying, repeating the only word she knew, 'Mm…ma!'

This was the opportunity that Hema had been waiting for. She picked up the jewellery on the floor, quickly passed Kausalai, ran down the steps and disappeared.

'If you ever come here again, you will see what kind of respect that awaits you!' Kausalai screamed after her venomously as she comforted the baby and entered the house.

Even though Kannan was under the control of his wife, he was usually not afraid of her. But, when he saw the look on her face, he was scared. Giving away what was hers to another woman made him feel very guilty. Even at that moment, he was under Hema's spell and thought that Kausalai was overreacting.

'How long has this outrage been going on?'

'What has happened? Why are you shouting like this? She came here to talk about the money matter and when I told her that you were not home, she was leaving.'

'I, too, have a brain. It was clearly written on both your faces! That donkey ran away! How can I not see what happened?'

'She's from a well-to-do family. Don't insinuate anything that didn't happen.'

'If she's a rich woman, let her keep it in her house. I know how to tame her arrogance. Why did she give you her jewellery? I'll let her brother know!'

'Go on, go tell her brother!'

'I *am* going!' she said, placing the crying baby on the floor as she left.

'Where are you going?' he said, blocking her way.

'You're the one who told me to! I'm going to demand justice from her brother. I going to say to him: "You're sending your sister out like this and ruining the town. Aren't you ashamed of yourself?"'

'Are you going to shut your mouth or not?'

'I will not. What are you going to do about it?'

Wordlessly, Kannan started repeatedly hitting her mouth, head, back and chest. Then, he kicked her. Kausalai was quite capable of screaming and attracting her neighbours' attention, but she felt so humiliated that she bore everything silently.

'Why don't you just kill me so you can go frolicking with that loose woman?'

'You spiteful bitch, shut your mouth!' he said as he kicked her again and left the house, feeling ashamed of himself.

## Chapter 25

It was well past ten o'clock by the time Kannan returned home. Until that day, he had never beaten his wife and was feeling miserable about it. When he approached his house, he saw something shining by the roadside and picked it up. It was Hema's bangle! He looked around carefully to make sure that there was nothing else left behind. When Hema had left in a hurry, she must have dropped this bangle. It was a good thing that he had found it! He tucked it around his waist.

*If our devil had found it, she would have been at it again! What a scene she created!* he fondly chastised her in his mind. *How am I going to pacify her?* Kannan thought and sighed. He did not feel bad that he had done something wrong; he only felt bad because Kausalai had found out. He neither could nor tried to forget Hema. He could still feel her refreshing presence all over him—just the thought of her gave him goosebumps. He was even feeling a bit afraid that Hema might be angry with him. He felt very sorry for Kausalai because he could not get Hema out of his mind.

Kausalai was fast asleep with the baby next to her. He gently prodded her and woke her up. Blood had oozed out of her mouth and dried over her chin. He held her affectionately and wiped it off with his veshti. He gently stroked her hair and said sympathetically, 'I hit you very hard, didn't I? You should not have created such a scene. Let it go! What happened regarding the matter that you had gone out about?'

'Nothing different from what happened here. There, my brothers beat each other up. My younger brother beat my elder brother for stealing the jewellery and money. My elder brother took aim with a crowbar. It was a good thing that there were others at home to hold him back.'

'All this happened before you got there?'

'That's right. When I got there, the Panchayat had already convened. No one was able to look the other in the face. I told them my grievance.'

'You shouldn't have.'

'I felt like it, so I did. Then, they called on my brothers and inquired about it. They were all in agreement that my father had never mentioned anything like that. At least on this one matter, they were unanimous!'

'Why create unnecessary displeasure?'

'What unnecessary displeasure? My younger sister-in-law said hurtful things to me, and I gave it back to her. I left without bidding farewell to anyone. After my father's death, what do I have left in that house?'

'So, you had to pick a fight for that reason? What has happened has happened.'

'A corpse can't return home. A broken pot can't be glued together—that's it!' said Kausalai, wiping her tears.

'Crazy! Why do we need their money?'

'I was not referring to that. I was talking about the drama you put on here!' said Kausalai, redirecting the conversation where Kannan had not expected it to go.

'Nothing happened. You're making a mountain out of a molehill—'

'Enough! Stop!' Kausalai interrupted Kannan.

He shut his mouth and thought it would be best to let her come to peace with it in her own way.

After a little while, Kausalai said, 'Listen to what I have to say. I have a gold chain around my neck worth a thousand rupees. Go sell it so we can get our house repaired. You can work fast. We'll run out of jari and silk, right?'

'Alright, tell me,' Kannan said.

'We don't need our own looms now. First, let's settle our debts, get two looms and work as wage labourers. I can weave on one of them.'

'You are pregnant. How can you work during this time?'

'I had forgotten about that! Alright then, you get a loom and work for someone else. When good times return, we can own our looms.'

'What you say is right. We can't manage with the loan,' said Kannan, agreeing with her. She spoke to him in her usual way, and it seemed like she had made peace with Kannan. It seemed like she had completely forgotten the incident with Hema. At the same time, the caring words that were flowing from her felt like heavy stones piling upon him. She was not speaking in riddles or trying to be smart, yet, Kannan felt that there was a deeper meaning in her words that he could not fathom.

'Raji is going to wake up, shall we sleep?' Kannan asked.

'It looks like you have not eaten. Come, I will serve you. The leftover rice I had soaked in water must have gotten too soggy. You might have to drink the gruel,' Kausalai responded.

'I'll eat only if you join me.'

'I will,' she agreed immediately.

Both finished eating in silence. She left the dirty pots and pans next to the tap and spread a single mat for him.

'Is one mat enough?' he asked laughing.

'I'm going to sleep there,' she said pointing to where the baby was asleep.

'How long do you think it will take me to come over there?'

'I'm sleeping over there because I don't want you near me.'

She slept next to the baby. He crept closer to her and when he touched her, she sprang up hissing like a snake. She turned on the lamp and said, 'Did you not understand what I said? Don't touch me! I have already warned you. Even looking at you makes me feel sick.'

She never mentioned Hema's name, but he realized that the incident had affected her deeply.

'I can't even *imagine* doing such a thing. Even thinking about it makes me feel sick in the stomach,' she said.

He was not surprised to see tears streaming down her face. But when she cast off her usual pleasant face and wore a grotesque expression, like the scary masks children wear, he felt afraid! He could not understand how a beautiful face like hers could contort into such ugliness within a few minutes. He began to wonder if she was possessed. The loneliness of the night made him feel even more afraid.

He could only beg her: 'Don't talk like that Kausalai!'

'Then why are you coming to me?'

To pacify her, he said, 'I won't. You go ahead and sleep!'

'Swear on your child!' she said, weeping.

He realized that this was the wrong time to be having a conversation with her and covered himself with his bedsheet. Although he badly wanted to comfort his weeping wife, he did not have the courage!

Kausalai continued to stand at the same spot. He closed his eyes and pretended to be asleep, but the lamp was still burning, and he knew that she was standing there like a figurine. He felt that there was darkness within the light and that was why he could not see her. His mother had passed away and then his father-in-law. So, he understood the heaviness in grieving for the departed. But, he felt that a more profound grief emanated from within Kausalai and filled the house. To forget the weight of all this sorrow, he redirected his mind towards happy thoughts. Hema appeared as the source of all his happy thoughts! *Could Kausalai not have come a little later?* Kannan thought, achingly.

The lamp continued to burn and Kausalai continued to stand there. Kannan was enjoying thoughts of Hema. The crickets were calling loudly. Baby Raji turned over and was sleeping on her back. Then, she started crying, 'Pa...pa!'

When the grief of her grandfather's passing had made her mother wail, she had uttered her first word, 'Amma.' What grief made her utter her second word 'Pa', now? Maybe she had opened her mouth to chastise her father's actions!

## Chapter 26

Jembu Rangasamy was cheerfully reciting a prayer when he arrived at Kannan's house. He participated in bhajans on a regular basis, and thus muttering them under his breath was a habit. His specialty was Saurashtrian bhajans. 'Kannan has been "summoned". The union president wants to see him,' he said.

Kausalai's face bore witness to the stress from the night before. Despite all that, without much exchange, she prepared idlis and coffee. Kannan had just finished his breakfast and stepped out of the kitchen.

As soon as Kausalai saw Rangan, her face twisted. He heard her muttering, 'The evil eye is here.'

'Come in Rangan, be seated!' said Kannan trying to drown Kausalai's words.

'Amma seems to get angry as soon as I arrive!' Rangan said.

'Angry? Look here! You kept praising and envying our house

and now it's in shambles. It looks like not even half the warp and jari can be salvaged. We're ready to pawn our jewellery to get the cash we need. Does that satisfy you?' Kausalai demanded, without even glancing at him.

Kannan felt awkward. 'Get back to your work, Kausalai! He just arrived and you're already picking a fight with him!' Kannan ordered.

Rangan was not the type to be fazed by such words. 'Let her say what she wants to. Am I going to be pleased by your downfall? Yes! It's going to be very profitable for me. My stomach will be full as well, right?' he said laughing.

'Do people get jealous because it's profitable for them? Some people just can't take it when others do well. If neighbours do well, they can't bear it. If a husband and wife get along well, they feel jealous! That is their nature. Even when we sit down for a meal, you are envious! We had a fight yesterday,' Kausalai retorted.

Kannan felt very uneasy. He did not want Kausalai to fight with Rangan, and if he allowed her to continue at this pace, he did not know what other information she might blurt out and embarrass him. 'Rangan, why did the president ask for me? I have urgent work and you are sitting here, relaxed,' he said as he grabbed Rangan's arm and marched towards the entrance.

'Husband and wife fight, huh? Am I the one who got caught in the middle of all this?' Rangan asked.

'Every household is bound to see its share of fights. Just be glad that you just had to hear that much. Now, let go of it and tell me: what did the president need me for?'

'He has been hollering, "Kanna, Kanna". But you don't come there anymore.'

'When you are well aware of everything that has happened to me recently, how can you say such things? Are Kausalai's views about you without any grounds?'

'She keeps beating you down because you keep putting her up on a pedestal.'

'Alright, I know that! I'm not like you to beat my wife! Tell me the matter you came about.'

'The president will explain everything. It looks like the muthalalis are going to wag their tails. This time, we should chop them off short!'

'If *we* are united, what can they do?'

'That's also right. Now, tell me something: you and Kausalai never fight. What happened all of a sudden?'

Kannan realized that Rangan's focus was still on his family discord. Kausalai was right after all—this was Rangan's true nature. 'Rangan, our Raji has started talking. She's calling us amma and appa now!'

'That's great news! Make a vow to tie a bell at the Amman Temple and she'll start speaking in no time!'

Rangan did not get any response to his malicious line of questioning. When they arrived at the union building, it was overflowing with weavers, and Kannan was welcomed enthusiastically. The president was in his office and gave Kannan a quick update.

The weavers' notice with their demands had reached the industrialists' association. The industrialists had convened a meeting to discuss the demands. They all agreed about not allowing a strike before Deepavali, but some did not agree with the demand for higher wages. 'When wages have not been raised in Kanchipuram, Arani and Thanjavur, it's not right to do so here,' they argued as usual. 'Let the weavers go on a strike and face the consequences,' a few of them fumed. But most of them did not share this view. 'When the costs are increasing on a daily basis, it's only right that wages should be raised,' many industrialists agreed. A few prominent ones even said, 'Let's raise the wages here and set an example for the other towns.' So, the issue became how much the wage increase should be. The weavers had demanded an increase of twenty-five per cent over the current rates, which all the industrialists unanimously agreed was way too high.

'If the weavers' union president and the president of the industrialists' association met, they would come to a reasonable decision,' the members of the industrialists' association determined. According to that decision, the president of the industrialists' association sent an invitation to Subburao, who wanted Kannan to accompany him.

If the weavers' president was a sharp man, would the industrialists' president be any less? Kanniyer, the president of the association, had over three hundred looms to his name. He was well known for his ability to trick weavers. He had both the financial might as well as the backing of a strong legal muscle. Just like Subburao, Kanniyer had been the president of the industrialists' association for a very long time.

'Kanniyer thinks that we are fools. We were fooled once before. We need to make sure that he understands that we're not going to be fooled again. He is apparently plotting to drag out the negotiations until Deepavali, as he believes that during that time, the weavers will accept whatever the muthalalis offer and settle,' said Subburao.

'He's right about that though. Let's not wait until then. We need to know their final decision either today or tomorrow. Otherwise, we should go on a token strike,' said Kannan.

'Apparently Kanniyer has said that they could create discord among the weavers. Let's put an end to his pipe dreams,' said Rangasamy.

The communist Balakrishnan spoke with his usual ferocity: 'Are we any less than the sanitary workers? When they stopped work for two days, the whole town was stinking! Did they not get everything that they demanded? You are making a mistake if you think that the muthalalis will give in.'

'If the muthalalis don't give in, I will go on a hunger strike—a fast unto death!' announced Dravida Kazhagam-supporter Ramamurthy.

Saranathan, who was also there, said: 'It's not sufficient for one person to go on a hunger strike. We have to make sure that at least four of us are starving in front of each muthalali's house. We shouldn't give a free pass to the bootlickers of the muthalalis and the scabs either. We should picket their houses as well.'

'Good idea! If we don't reach an amicable solution today, we need to step up our activism. We're ready for a compromise and I have a feeling that we're going to succeed,' said Kannan.

'*Compromise?* See what you'll get: they're going to pour pepper rasam in your eyes!' Saranathan warned.

'What's this? We're trying to negotiate a settlement and you're cursing us?'

'If we go back and forth like this, we're not going to come to a final decision. If there was a strike that would not be a big problem for the muthalalis, but it would be perilous for us.'

'Only when we go back and forth like this can we elicit everyone's views on this matter. We'll ultimately be bound by the decision of our president.'

'Long live President Subburao!' everyone exclaimed.

Many were heard bidding them farewell as Subburao and Kannan left the building. Kannan and Subburao met the industrialists' association's president at his house. He spoke pleasantly, with a smile on his face, and emphasized the reasonable nature of the demands put forward by the weavers. He vehemently condemned the government for not controlling prices and said that the present government should be taught a lesson in the next election. 'I agree with everything, but the weavers demand for a twenty-five per cent increase in wages is not right,' said Kanniyer and showed them the accounts for silk, jari, interest and so forth. 'If we raise the wages above five per cent, the whole weaving industry will come to a grinding halt,' he said.

Subburao's response was calmer and more succinct than that of Kanniyer. He had made a note of the food prices. He explained how much a family would make in a month even if all of them wove for a living. Even if you raise a quarter rupee per rupee, they can't make ends meet. Therefore, we can't lower our demand,' he said firmly.

'I'm not saying that your demand is unfair, but the industry has to survive as well, right? I can't make this decision unilaterally. We're calling an administrative committee meeting next week and will be sending you an invitation. Please come, and we can come to a sensible arrangement.' It was very clear that Kanniyer was employing delaying tactics.

Kannan said: 'We've agreed to be bound by our president's decision. Similarly, we assumed that your association would have given you the authority to negotiate on their behalf. If not, what's the point of negotiating with you?' Kannan asked defiantly.

Kannan's talk irritated Kanniyer: 'That's right! The association *has* given me the authority, but does that mean I can decide according to my wishes?'

'Haven't they given you the authority because they trust your decisions? Didn't you just agree that the weavers' demands were fair? Based on the daily trials of the poor, if you make a just decision, the others will not disagree,' said Kannan.

'You don't understand the muthalalis. They will let you move forward, and then they'll pull the rug out from under your feet. Next week, the administrative committee meeting is being held. If you'll come, we can reach a decision.'

'Deepavali is almost here, and we can't afford to keep postponing this by a week at a time like this. That would leave the weavers with very little choice,' Kannan said.

'The deadline announced through our notice ends today. If we don't get your final decision by today, we will be forced to begin a token strike according to the unanimous decision taken by our members. What can I do beyond that?' asked Subburao.

'In my opinion, you don't need to go on a strike at all. If you can hold off for a week, I can try to convince the other muthalalis to agree to a wage increase. Even if they don't agree to a twenty-five per cent increase, I'll urge them to agree to something fair. This is a serious matter. We shouldn't do anything in a hurry. After all, Deepavali comes annually. Should we take such a big decision in a hurry because of that?' Kanniyer said.

The negotiations that began in the afternoon, thus, continued without an accord until evening. Finally, Subburao expressed his position: 'I'm bound by the decisions of my union. There's going to be a token strike tomorrow.'

'Go ahead. Maybe the muthalalis might even change their minds because of that. Then, my work will be easy!' said Kanniyer, as usual, speaking soothingly with the workers.

Thus, the negotiations broke down!

The news spread like wildfire. A huge crowd gathered at the union. No one was to go to work the next day. A procession and a meeting emphasizing the demands of the workers were planned. The president, Kannan and a few other important organizers did not go home that night and stayed on to organize the following day's events.

The president strictly prohibited the use of all slogans that could aggravate the simmering anger; he also listed all the slogans that were to be chanted. Since the general election was fast approaching, the ruling party would be interested in obtaining the weavers' votes. So, Kannan suggested that they chant slogans that would attract the attention of the ruling party. Subburao endorsed this idea. Placards with slogans such as 'Give us a kilo of rice!', 'Reduce the prices of food items!', 'Increase our wages!' were raised.

No weaver went to work the next day. Many women and children joined the protest march, which was about a mile long. The procession began at four in the evening. Rangasamy led the bhajan contingent. Balakrishnan, Ramamurthy and Saranathan roared the slogans incessantly. The march began at the Ramasamy Temple and snaked through the important streets, ending in Thuvarankurichi at nine in the night.

The stage and microphone had already been set up. Subburao gave a brief speech describing the negotiations he had had with Kanniyer. 'Today's token strike should be a warning for the industrialists,' he said.

Kannan, too, spoke to the weavers. 'If the government doesn't intervene and deliver a just solution, it'll face the wrath of the weavers. The problems faced by the silk weavers are different from those faced by the cotton weavers. Subsequent governments have ignored silk weavers. At least, now they should address our problems on a humanitarian basis,' Kannan said.

A few other notable members of the union spoke as well. The meeting ended after delegating the responsibility and authority to the president to proceed with the subsequent necessary actions.

## Chapter 27

By the time the meeting ended and everyone dispersed, it was eleven in the night. Kannan and a few others had stayed back to return the borrowed tables and chairs to their rightful owners and dismantle the stage. So, when Kannan finally bade farewell to the president and left the venue, it was past midnight. As all his friends had already left, he was all alone.

He felt he could have spoken better at the meeting and wished he could speak fluently like Balakrishnan. At the same time, he also felt excessive emotion was not right. As long as the muthalalis agreed, everything was going to be good. What other option did they have anyway?

Now, what was Kausalai going to say when he returned home? It had been over two days since he had seen her. Might her anger have subsided by now? He had just understood her keen sense of honour. *She had thrown a fit as if her family's ancestral heirloom had been looted*, Kannan thought and laughed to himself.

He was passing Koththan Street and was walking very slowly, as he was sleepy and tired and his thoughts were weighing him down. He heard someone calling him from behind, and he turned around. It did not take him long to recognize Hema.

'What are you doing out at this time of the night?' he asked as she approached him.

'I came to hear you speak. You spoke very well,' she responded.

Her courage astonished him. He also felt very happy knowing that he was the cause of her courage. To be honest, as soon as he saw her, his fatigue vanished and he felt energized. The slight chill he had been feeling also disappeared and he warmed up!

'Let's put the discussion about my speech aside. It's so late, isn't anyone going to look for you at your house?'

'I told my mother before I left.'

They spoke while looking at each other in the illumination of the streetlight under which they stood. He was afraid that someone else might see them. He moved towards a darker area. She followed and stood right by him as if asserting her right to be close to him. When her hands came in contact with his, his heart leapt as if someone had pinched it.

'You have courage. What did you tell your mother? Did you say you were going to listen to me speak?'

'Why would I say that? I told her that I wanted to observe

the meeting. My mother knows how to manage these things. Why did Kausalai get so angry?'

'Wouldn't one get very angry?'

'She has no pity. What has she lost? I would never betray her. Did she fight with you after I left?'

'Fight with me? It was war! She said just the sight of me made her sick and shouted at me not to touch her. She stood awake all night in case I touched her.'

'Oh, what a pity! She should be fine in four days or so, right?'

'We're standing in the middle of the street. What if someone sees us?' Kannan said apprehensively.

'I can't come to your house. I am unable to go on without seeing you. Tell me a way to see you,' Hema whined.

Kannan, too, was overcome with longing. 'Tomorrow is the eighth day after my father-in-law's death. Kausalai will be going to her family home. Come around noon and leave quickly, alright? You want too much!'

'It's all because of you! You have wrecked my heart! I'm always thinking about you. How long do you want to stand here and talk to me? Where can we go now?'

'Right now?'

'Yes, *right now!*'

Kannan was the ruler, but in that moment, he felt that he was being ruled by Hema: 'Where can one go at this time of the night? I am very tired, as I didn't sleep well last night. The last two days have been very hectic.'

'Yes, when I call you, you are tired or sleepy. Go home and

sleep!' she said, pretending to pull away from him.

'I couldn't even pacify one woman, and now you have become cantankerous! So, tell me, where do you want to go?'

'Let's go to the riverside. It's a moonlit night! We can talk for a little while.'

'To the riverside? Don't we have to pass the children's cemetery to get there? Aren't you afraid of *anything*?'

'With you by my side, what's there to be afraid of?'

Both of them walked in the dark and reached the riverside. In the moonlight, the river seemed to be floating. Because of the chill in the air, even the trees seemed to be breathing heavily. The birds had retreated to their nests. As soon as they had their privacy, in the absence of any ears or eyes, Hema warmed to Kannan. She caressed him and erased his fatigue as he sat on the embankment.

'You dropped one of your bangles when you ran away the other day. I'll give it to you when you come tomorrow.'

'I don't need my bangle back. Keep it. I anyway thought I had lost it. My only concern was to escape from Kausalai! She seems so passive, but that night, she started screaming like a devil. Is labelling me as a loose woman acceptable? Ask her that. Have you found a person to repair the house?'

'Every day the mason says that he will come over but has not turned up for four days. Masons and carpenters are in demand these days and only weavers like us have become cheap.'

'You got the money by pawning the warp and jari, right? You keep this,' Hema said, handing Kannan one of her gold chains, 'it's about five sovereigns worth. Use it to redeem the silk and jari. I am getting a minor chain[36] made for you!'

'What is all this? I don't want anything. To accept it would be humiliating for me.'

'Do you find it humiliating to take things from me? Have I become a stranger to you all of a sudden?'

'Is that what all this means?'

'I want to adorn you. What's that to you? It's *my* wish!'

'What!? You are creating unnecessary trouble for me. If I put on a show all of a sudden, what will others think of me?'

'What does it matter what others think of us? I don't want you coming outside without a shirt from now on! The saying goes that even if you are hit by a stone don't get caught by someone's evil eyes.'

'I can see how profitable this is when one is seen by greedy eyes.'

'Of course, you will say that. Why wouldn't you? Hold my hand and promise me that you will not betray me or Kausalai!'

'You keep on rambling!'

'Are you afraid to promise me? Alright, no need then; just tell me that you will not cheat—that's enough.'

'Why are you doubting me to be a traitor?'

'Like me, I don't know how many people's hearts you are going to wreck!'

---

[36] A gold chain worn around the neck by men, sometimes derogatorily referred to as a minor chain. A philanderer is referred to as a minor in Tamil.

'Did I wreck it?'

'No, I ruined it myself! I have gone crazy!'

'You are just giving away your jewellery. Wouldn't someone ask about it at home?'

'Who dares to ask me? They are living off my money. Didn't my elder brother ruin my life? He married me off to a dying man because he was rich. Was that fair? If it were his daughter, would he have done that? If he challenges me, I, too, have a few things to ask him. I have no other option; I am in love with you. If I make a mistake beyond that, you can beat me with your slippers. If my brother asks, I am not going to let go of it—is his wife a proper woman? She also has eyes for you!'

'Eyes for me!'

Yes, yes. You don't know your reputation. No need to lose your head over that now!'

'I am only listening to what you have to say.'

'That's why I want to adorn and admire you, alright? Just say yes.'

'Hmm...alright!'

'Make peace with Kausalai. I want to have a good relationship with her so that I can come to your house whenever I want to.'

'I don't think that's going to happen. I was really afraid the other night. She's a very proud woman!'

'You can do it. You have charmed me! Do you think you can't make Kausalai change her mind? Get her some jewellery and silk saris. You know the rest! I don't need to teach you that.'

'Nothing that I can do will make her change her mind. She

is already like a madwoman. I am so afraid to go home now, not knowing what she is going to say!'

'With time, everything will be alright. Until then, do we have to keep meeting secretly like this?'

'What other option do we have?'

'By the riverside, under the moonlit sky! If I had known, I would've brought some snacks. Won't you talk to me?'

'You talk non-stop!'

'Say something!'

Kannan remained silent.

'Talk!'

Silence.

'You won't talk to me?'

Still, silence.

'Oh, God!'

## Chapter 28

When Kannan finally woke up the next morning, he was exhausted. Every joint in his body was aching. He felt as if Hema was by him, but when he realized that he was home, he tried to remember when he had returned. Then it all came back to him. Hema and he had parted with anguish. Then, his stream of consciousness had continued on his way home: Kausalai, the baby and so on. He wondered whether he had overslept and called out from his sleeping mat, 'Kausalai, what time is it?'

'It's past eleven,' Kausalai responded.

'*Eleven*! Shouldn't you have woken me up?'

'Why would I wake you up? You only got back early in the morning. I didn't want to wake you so that you could get some sleep.'

'Yes, by the time the meeting ended, it was midnight. After that, we had to return the various things we had borrowed to their owners. Once their business was over, everyone vanished, so the president and I had to take care of everything. Can you just leave after that? We continued talking and didn't realize that the hours had flown by.'

He thought that he had given her an adequate excuse for returning home late. She responded from the kitchen: 'Yes, I heard that you have been very busy the past two days. As long as you were helpful to others—it's good.'

He felt that Kausalai's responses were contrived. He did not think that she would have found out about the previous night. No one had seen them. It was the lingering effect of the old grievance that was making her behave unlike herself, he guessed.

'What's Raji doing?'

'What else does she do? Surprisingly, two words have gotten stuck in her mouth and she keeps shouting 'Paa' and 'Amma'.'

Kausalai gave him his coffee, and as he drank it, he picked up the baby.

'Someone came from the union. The president has asked you to come at five in the evening.'

'Did Rangan come with the message?' he asked as he sat down next to her and continued, 'any other news?'

'It wasn't Rangan. Someone new. Members of the Congress Party have come, and they want to hold peace talks in the evening.'

'Oh, they have come, have they? I thought they might! It is election time, so even if we don't get everything that we demand, they'll come to a reasonable decision, you'll see!'

'If they raise the wages, wouldn't it be a loss for you?'

'How so? You're the one who told me to work on a loom as a wage worker. It's good if the wages rise, right?'

'Why should you be a wage worker? You are going to become a muthalali.'

'You keep on saying contradictory things. You are holding on to one topic and not letting go!'

'You can't let it go and neither can I. You have figured out a way to make quick money. Make a lot of money and live well. As long as you are happy!'

Kannan began to have doubts as to why she was talking like this. When her expression began to twist, just like the other night, he felt afraid again despite it being daytime.

'I don't know how to make quick money. I do it by weaving a stitch at a time,' Kannan said.

'You don't want that life anymore!' Kausalai responded.

'Why are you talking like this?'

'Even if you wish to, is Hema going to allow it? She's a rich woman. She's not going to allow you to be a weaver!'

'What do we care if she is rich? You're the one who was trying to get close to her. Now, you're saying all sorts of things. Why is she going to come here?'

'Why does she have to come *here*? You'll go where she is!'

'Did you sit down with the intent of picking a fight with me? Will you not believe what I say?'

'Alright, tell me.'

'She's not more important to me than you. Let's not fight

over that donkey. Even if I see her in the future, I will not speak to her, alright?' Kannan reassured Kausalai.

'Are you done speaking? I believe you!' she said while laughing.

'You are speaking with something weighing on your mind,' Kannan said with concern.

'I'm not hiding anything. Look at this!' she said, laying Hema's bangles and her thick rope necklace in front of him! He had hidden them well in the almirah drawer. How had she found them?

'Last evening, I saw the bangles. Now, the necklace has appeared. You carefully hid them from me, but God has given me eyes to see all this! Hema gave this to you last night, didn't she? If she becomes your wife, would she give them to you? Will she be this loving?'

Kannan had wanted to pacify Kausalai, but now, all he wanted was to escape from her. 'You'll keep saying something or other. If you want to find something wrong, you always can.'

'I didn't say anything was wrong. Initially, I thought it was wrong and it was my fault for thinking that. You think that I am going to fight with you like the other day, right? But I'll not fight with you again.'

Kannan did not say anything. He had been hoping that she would calm down and show them a way out of this mess.

'The other day, I uttered whatever came to my mouth to Hema. Poor thing! I feel that was wrong of me!'

'She's still very fond of you,' he said inadvertently and stopped at that.

'Of course, she's going to be fond of me. Why wouldn't she? She found you because of me, right? There's nothing wrong. You need two hands to clap. Can you just blame one hand? I was wrong; I cursed *her*! You tell her that. Since she gave you jewellery, she must have said that she would give me some as well? She must have told you that. Don't try to hide it from me. She must even have said that we could all three live happily together!'

He had not expected her to know exactly what had transpired between him and Hema the previous night. She spoke as if she had been at the riverside, listening to him and Hema! She was not speaking like a human being but like an all-knowing monster. Her face! Even the sound of her words was sucking his blood dry. She was killing him.

'I promise I'll not look at her again. Please be your usual self, Kausalai!'

'You must've promised her as well? Don't you have to keep that promise, too?'

'I've just had my coffee. It's time for breakfast. You keep on going like this!' Kannan started raising his voice.

'I already told you that I will not fight with you. As long as you are happy, everything is alright. I came to this decision only this morning. You returned home stealthily early in the morning, made sure no one was looking when you hid the gold necklace, and then went to sleep. As soon as you lay down, you were snoring. You were exhausted! The sound of your snoring fuelled my rage. I was disgusted as well. I came and sat next to you. Do you know what I felt like doing at that moment? I felt like strangling you! I would have, but I felt sorry for you. Killing one's husband is very sinful! I felt really bad that I had devilishly even considered killing you. But I can't even look at you anymore. You are part of me, like the salt of my body. Now, even my body disgusts me! This baby is here because of you. Even touching or looking at her makes me sick to the stomach.'

Her words were crushing him, but he did not know how to stop her. *If she continues like this for a few more minutes, I am going to die!* Kannan thought, feeling exhausted.

'Is Raji asleep? Let me have her back so that my filth stays with me!' she said, grabbing the baby, before she added, 'Am I fighting with you? No. You're not going to be angry with me, are you?'

'I'm not angry. You are pregnant and if you torment your mind like this, what'll happen to you?' Kannan asked, concerned.

'I keep forgetting that I'm pregnant! There is another ugliness growing inside me. How can I endure all this?' she said, bursting out crying.

'What you are doing to yourself is very good!'

'Why did my father have to die now? How did he have the heart to leave me alone like this?'

'Do people die because they choose to? Old age—'

'He died because he wanted to make me suffer, but I'm going to dupe him. I'm not going to suffer anymore. I'm going to be happy, alright?' she said, laughing.

'Why are you laughing like that?'

Her silence felt like the speech had come to a full stop.

'It's two o'clock, Kausalai!'

'Yes, it's very late. I have to go to my father's house. You should have a bath. As usual, you can serve yourself food. I am leaving.'

'It's quite late. Why don't you serve my food and eat with me before leaving?'

'No, I'm not hungry. What will the others think? Shall I take your leave now?' she asked as she stood up.

'Eat before you leave, Kausalai.'

'No, it's already late.'

'Can't you at least serve me food before leaving?'

'You are being obstinate, like a child! Haven't you served yourself before? Today is the eighth day after my father's death. If I'm not there, even if my brothers don't say anything, others will. I'm going. You should bathe and then eat.'

In that moment, he thought that it would be best for her to leave. He would not be able to restore her deranged mind today. He also had not forgotten that Hema was going to come over that afternoon. If that out-of-control woman arrived now—no need for any more trouble!

It did not seem like Kausalai was expecting his response. She took Hema's bangle and necklace, went to the almirah and stood there fiddling around for a little while. Then, she placed the baby over her shoulder to sleep.

'Have a bath and eat, alright? Don't torment yourself. You

should live happily, alright?' she said as she left.

Even though she was going to her parent's house, part of him felt like dragging her back and tying her up. At the same time, he knew that if Hema arrived, it would be disastrous. He went to the front porch and watched her until she disappeared over the horizon.

*Let her go. Once she has a good cry there, she will feel better,* thought Kannan as he entered the house. The house did not feel like a home anymore. He felt all alone in an open space, with nothing beyond the horizon.

He did not feel like taking a bath or eating. Then, he remembered that Hema was coming over and his heart started to pound. He felt disgusted about showing his face to her and decided to leave before she arrived. He quickly put on his shirt, locked the door and left. The union president had wanted him to come at five in the evening, but he decided to go right away and wait for him. All he wanted was to escape from those female devils!

## Chapter 29

Subburao's sole focus at that point was to resolve the weavers' problem. He stood talking to some union members.

'Not gone home yet?' Kannan asked him.

'I did—I just returned. Our strategy is working. Muthaiya and Yakub woke me up this morning. "Don't aggravate the situation," they requested. Then, they went to see Kanniyer,' Subburao explained. Muthaiya was the head of the Congress Party in their town and Yakub was a party veteran.

'If they take a unilateral decision and then try to control us—'

Subburao laughed, interrupting Kannan. 'They seem more determined to get fair wages for the weavers than we are! If we reach an amicable solution, the Congress Party can be proud of its achievement and, in return, can ask for our vote, right?'

'What do you expect will come out of it?'

'If it's below fifteen per cent, let's not be bound by it, alright?'

'It's Deepavali time. If the industrialists agree to fifteen per cent, it's good.'

'Something wrong with your health?'

'Not at all!'

'You look out of sorts. Have you eaten?'

Only then did Kannan remember that he had not eaten. His stomach had gone numb with hunger. As soon as he had some hot coffee and snacks, he felt rejuvenated. He had never imagined that Kausalai could get so angry and talk like this. He usually knew how to entice her, but with all the additional work that had piled on him, he had not found time to speak to her at leisure. Hopefully, the wage dispute would be resolved today. It *will* be resolved—it had to be! Then, before anything else, he would make peace with Kausalai, poor thing. She was kneading her heart like dough. Would Hema have arrived after he left for the union? She was quite crazy! She, doubtlessly, must have come. When she must have seen the door locked, she must have felt let down and returned home, poor thing.

The union was surging with people. They were sharing their many points of view and all of them were eagerly awaiting a fair solution. Past five o'clock, when there was no news forthcoming from the Congress leaders, the situation became a bit shaky. 'We need to plan our next steps,' some of the leftists said impatiently. But, Subburao did not budge, and his conviction was not in vain. Just past six o'clock, an invitation arrived.

Once again, mediation talks resumed at the industrialists' association's President Kanniyer's house. Along with Kanniyer, a few other big industrialists were present at the meeting. Only Subburao and Kannan represented the weavers and neither said much. Subburao sat indifferently as if he held the trump card. Both Muthaiya and Yakub spoke in support of the weavers. Due to their insistence, the industrialists offered a ten per cent increase, but Subburao insisted on twenty per cent.

At that point, it seemed like the talks were going to break down. Kanniyer was hesitating, but Kannan noticed that he and the other industrialists were respectful towards Muthaiya. *They are from the ruling party. If the weavers' issue becomes a political problem, there will be problems in the industry*, thought the industrialists.

Muthaiya took advantage of this favourable moment. 'Both sides have to give in. It is only fair that the industrialists give in more. Are the weavers going to put their money in a fixed deposit account in the bank? Industrialists are worried that their profits will be less, but the weavers are worried about getting a single square meal a day. The industry must go on. I will decide on behalf of both parties, but both sides have to agree. So, can we have a fifteen per cent wage increase starting tomorrow? Kanniyer? Say yes! Subburao! Alright?' said Muthaiya, trying to end the negotiations.

The industrialists were murmuring amongst themselves. 'You don't understand the problems in this industry. Fifteen per cent is going to be very difficult for us,' began Kanniyer.

'I have been told by the union not to agree to anything less than twenty per cent,' said Subburao calmly.

'If you start with a strike, this and that, it is going to be a loss for everyone. Both parties should accept my decision,' said Muthaiya.

Though they continued to argue for a little while longer, finally, everyone accepted his decision. The negotiation ended with both parties reaching a written agreement.

As soon as the matter was resolved, the tension in the atmosphere vanished. Everyone started laughing and talking. Coffee and snacks arrived from a restaurant. By the time everyone finished and left, it was past ten o'clock in the night.

Muthaiya dropped off Subburao and Kannan at the union office in his car. The weavers were waiting to hear the final agreement. On Subburao's request, Muthaiya made the announcement. The weavers were content with the decision. No one knew where the garlands came from, but Subburao, Muthaiya and Yakub were garlanded from head to foot. 'Long live Subburao! Long live Muthaiya!' the weavers thundered. A few of them even shouted 'Long live Kannan!'

Kannan was returning home with the satisfaction of having achieved something good. He could not decide whether Subburao or Muthaiya had been smarter. Muthaiya had won with his words, but Subburao had won without saying much. In the end, the weavers got justice.

On the way home, some of his friends stopped him to find out what each one of them had said during the peace talks. He gave appropriate answers to each of them as he walked. This world lives on its stomach. When the weavers found out they were going to get two meals a day, how their faces glowed!

When he realized that he had played a part in their joy, he felt energized. *I need to let Kausalai know. She will be happy as well. I should take this opportunity to resolve our family squabble,* he thought as he reached home.

The door was still locked. Why had Kausalai not come back? It was almost midnight. She had never stayed away this late! Since she had been angry when she left, maybe she had stayed at her parents' house.

He unlocked the door and went inside. The euphoria that he had felt on the way back evaporated. He felt as if someone had leapt on him and stabbed him in the back. The long hours, the back and forth and the exhaustion and exhilaration brought on by Hema began to weigh on him. He had a roaring headache. His head felt heavy, his heart began to ache and all he wanted to do was lie down where he was standing and fall asleep. But, how was he to sleep without Kausalai in the house?

Only a few minutes had passed, but it felt like hours. In the morning, Kausalai had rambled on and on, the proud woman! Does one have to be *so* lofty? She had even been ready to kill him! She had been hurt deeply. *I need to pacify Kausalai, cut off ties with Hema and toss her jewellery back at her. I should not see her ever again. Devil, devil!* Kannan thought.

He remembered that when Kausalai had put away Hema's jewellery in the almirah, she had been fiddling around for a while. What had she been up to?

He opened the almirah and pulled out the drawer. Hema's bangle and necklace lay right on top. Underneath that, there was a handkerchief and the jewellery that Kausalai had been wearing: necklaces, earrings, nose ring, the baby's necklace and two rings! Kannan's hands began to tremble, but he continued to look. The thaali[37] that he had fastened around her neck was there too! Yes, it was Kausalai's thaali!

What did this mean? Had she renounced him and gone back to her family? Who did she have there? She had gotten into a fight with her brothers as well. What was going on? What was Kausalai up to? What had she done? What had the wretch done?

Terror struck him. He felt as if his heart was bursting. He locked the front door and rushed to Thuvarankurichi. There, too, the door was bolted! He banged on the door, and his elder brother-in-law opened it.

'Oh, brother-in-law?' he said, surprised to see Kannan there.

'Is Kausalai here?' Kannan asked.

'Kausalai? She didn't even come today!'

'Didn't come?' Kannan collapsed on the porch. 'She left our house in the afternoon.'

'She didn't come here at all!'

'Where would she have gone?'

The other brothers-in-law and their wives joined.

---

[37] Married women wear it until their husband dies.

Consternation ensued. 'Have you two been fighting?' everyone kept asking.

'Fighting? What's there to fight between us? I've been very busy with union work. I've not taken care of her. Where could she have gone? Maybe—'

'Did she take the baby?' one of Kausalai's family members asked.

'No, the baby is tucked inside my shirt!' Kannan responded sarcastically.

'Brother-in-law, don't get agitated! Where's she going to go? Let's go back home and ask around,' one of Kausalai's brothers said.

Kannan felt as if he was sleepwalking. It felt like Kausalai was hammering on his chest! Both his brothers-in-law accompanied him as he started looking for her. When they reached the street, neighbours woke up and gathered around them.

'Kausalai? I saw her in town this evening with the baby,' one of them said.

'When I went to buy betel leaves, I saw her on Kumbeswaran North Street. I'm sure it was her,' another neighbour added.

Then came the shocking news.

'Behind the Big Temple, there is a golden waterlily pond, right? Kausalai was seated there with her baby. It was Kausalai. I looked carefully. I thought she was amusing the baby,' a third neighbour added.

Everything became very clear to Kannan now. He silently walked towards the golden waterlily pond. A big crowd followed him.

They looked around the pond. They even looked in the nooks and crannies of the temple hall. When they could not find her, they went to a nearby police station. The policeman who accompanied them back to the pond used a flashlight to inspect it. One constable dived into the pond. Some young men followed him.

Kannan sat in the hall. 'Kausalai has left with the baby. Does she have so much pride?' he was mumbling to himself.

Despite all the torment, the golden waterlily pond was silent all night. At the crack of dawn, it revealed its dark secret.

A woman's body floated up, holding a baby tightly to its chest.

## Chapter 30

Everything was conducted with propriety. Due to the intervention of dignitaries such as Subburao and Muthaiya, the police did not subject Kannan to the usual intense investigation. The death was recorded as a suicide due to unbearable stomach pains.

Both the bodies were taken to the hospital, and as if the suffering they had endured in the pond was not enough, they had to endure more. The bodies were taken directly from the hospital to the cemetery. The elders advised against taking the bodies back home due to the nature of their death.

Kannan, who had collapsed at his father-in-law's funeral, did not even cry this time. He merely stared at everything as if he had gone mad. He did whatever he was instructed to do. He seemed unaware of his actions. The priest kept reciting the prayers, but Kannan did not even move his lips. When he failed to do so, the others had to grab the rice, sesame seeds and khus grass in Kannan's hand and drop it on his behalf during the funeral ceremony. They had to repeatedly ask him to bathe when he got into the Kaveri River to be cleansed.

After finishing the last rites, they returned home around seven o'clock in the evening. At home, there was a big crowd including his brothers, sisters-in-law, sisters, children and brothers-in-law from Kausalai's family. He hardly spoke to anyone because he felt there was no one to speak to. He pretended to eat and slid into a deep slumber with an exhausted body and mind.

When he woke up the next morning, he had some clarity. After living the life of a family man, now he was back to being a bachelor again! Neither Kausalai nor Raji were there anymore. *The wretch! Could she not have at least left the baby?* Kannan thought resentfully. But when Kausalai was not there, what would happen to the baby?

It was all over. What was there to think about after everything had ended? Emptiness started to weigh his heart down as if it was clinging on to his chest, just as Kausalai had been holding on to Raji. What a difficult time they had had separating the two bodies!

As soon as the second-day rituals were over, Kausalai's relatives returned to their homes directly from the cemetery. What bonds existed between Kannan and them after Kausalai's demise?

Kannan's siblings and relatives camped at his house. Whether it was a wedding or a funeral, there was bound to be food. Just because someone has passed away, were others going to settle for something less? The house was full of people, bustling with many sounds.

Kannan was sickened by it all. There was not a single person in that crowd with whom he could speak confidentially. He felt like talking about Kausalai and Raji, but there was not a soul who could listen to him sympathetically and give him the comfort he needed. All of them were his siblings or relatives, and yet, they were the kind who lament for money. Family and relationships! All that ended with Kausalai. There was nothing left in this world for him.

On the afternoon of the second day after the deaths, Kannan saw everyone relishing the sambar and rasam, and he felt disgusted. When others spoke, it sounded like noise, and the cries of babies sounded like nails being driven into his ears. *They are not going to leave on their own. I have to chase them out,* Kannan decided.

'Others have left, aren't you going to leave?' he asked his eldest brother.

His brother was not expecting this question. 'We didn't come here to feast. We stayed on to support you. If you don't like it, we'll leave,' he said, with the sadness of being disrespected.

'He'll talk like that, but it will be wrong to leave him alone in this state,' said the sister who had come from the next town to be with her brother until everything was over.

'Why, do you think that I am going to hang myself? I'm

not going to do anything like that. I am unable to bear all this merriment. It will do if you all return for the tenth-day ceremonies,' Kannan retorted.

'Why should we even bother to come for that?' asked one of his sisters-in-law maliciously.

'As you wish,' Kannan said, without emotion.

'Elder brother is a rich man now. He married into a wealthy family. We are, after all, poor people. He doesn't care for us!' said Kannan's younger sister sarcastically.

Very soon, the house emptied and that began to torment Kannan. *I shouldn't have chased them away like that*, he thought regretfully. The silence pressed against him. It was difficult even to breathe as if something was blocking him from the inside. He walked around in circles inside the house. Was this not a ruined house? Once upon a time, he had dreamt of owning his home. After ruining all his relationships, was it still a home? What was the use of these bricks and sand? If Kausalai was here, as his wife, and Raji, as his baby, these stones and sand would have life. Now, they were ruins!

How long could he circle the room? Exhausted, he slumped down on the floor to sleep. He covered his face with a piece of cloth. They called it the corpse that fell in the water—that is right. How ghastly Kausalai and Raji looked! The corpses bloated, their eyes pecked out and lips torn by fish. Aiyyo! Even thinking about it was scary! Had Kausalai drowned herself to frighten him?

Kausalai and Raji in the water.

Kannan just could not imagine it. He gasped for breath. He tried breathing through his mouth, but he started choking. His limbs shook involuntarily.

'Pa…pa!' he heard the baby's lisp.

'I am calling you!' he heard Kausalai calling.

'Kausalai!' he called out, sobbing.

It was pitch dark, and it did not even occur to Kannan to turn on the light. What was the light going to reveal anyway?

He heard someone pushing the front door open, and then locking it behind them. He was sure who it was. Only one person had the courage to feel entitled to enter his house.

'Who's there?' he called softly.

'It's me,' he heard Hema's voice respond.

*What obstinacy! She needs to be kicked out. She needs to be skinned alive. That is not enough! She needs to be slowly tortured to death*, Kannan thought.

'Why have you come here? Leave!' Kannan ordered.

Silently, she came and sat next to him.

'After doing everything you did, what guts you have to come here!' he continued.

Even then, she did not respond and began to caress his chest gently. How did she figure out that all his grief was bundled up in his chest? Soon, his chest relaxed, and he was able to breathe again.

He thought of shoving her hand away, but his entire body resisted the thought. His body wanted her to continue caressing his chest.

'You should go away!' he repeated.

'I didn't come here to go away,' Hema finally responded.

'Have you come to stay with me?'

'Yes. Who else do you have now?'

'That's something!'

'I never thought that Kausalai would do such a thing. With one child at her bosom and the other in her womb, how did she have the heart to do it?'

Her warm tears fell on Kannan's chest. In that warmth, he felt a bond with her. When you have a ripe abscess and you try to break it, it hurts, right? But, if you apply a warm compress to it, the pain subsides, right? Kannan received that comfort from Hema's presence. He could kick her! He could also cry his heart out to her. He finally felt that someone close to him had arrived.

'All this happened because of your actions!' Kannan accused her.

'Everyone is saying that. You can too!' Hema replied defiantly.

'What's everyone saying?'

'That it all happened because of me. You were like a madman and didn't notice anything. On the first day, I came to the cemetery. Everyone was pointing at me and talking. Your younger sister made sure I heard her calling me a prostitute. I didn't say anything. You looked terrible. I felt scared to stay there, so I returned home.'

'After all this, why did you come here?'

'How can I not come? Everyone seems to know about our meeting by the riverside as well. If Kausalai was here, we would have to be secretive. She's gone. How can I leave you alone like this now? You have been confronted with so much grief! Don't I feel it too? Did I come to you for pleasure?'

She massaged his entire body and cracked his knuckles as she continued, 'Do you think I don't understand how much this hurts you? I, too, couldn't bear it. I didn't wish to betray her. Raji was like my own. I wanted Kausalai to be happy. I wanted you to be happy. I wished to see you both happy together and feel the joy of that. What's wrong with that?'

His head was on her lap and she was caressing his cheeks. When her breath touched him, he felt as if a primitive animal awoke inside him. Her touch captivated him. He also realized that these emotions released him from the enormous grief of Kausalai's loss. He wrapped his right hand around her hip.

'There's nothing wrong. This is right for both of us. Saying that is also wrong. This is the way out for us. We like the gutters and the stench. For Kausalai, the gutters were gutters and the stench was stench. She couldn't bear the ugliness, so she left!' Kannan said and started weeping. The grief of Kausalai melted and flowed as tears.

Hema affectionately held his head against her chest. When she wiped his tears, her tears wet his forehead. Only tears could ease tears; only grief comforted grief. This was not a court held by the God of Death or an inquiry into right or wrong. It was a woman and a man finding gratification amidst human needs of hunger, thirst, desire and affection.

Eventually, they stopped weeping. Their accumulated grief scattered. It felt as if a gentle breeze had wafted in during intense heat.

'Something that should never have happened has happened. What are you going to do now?' Hema asked Kannan.

'I want to go looking for Kausalai, but I don't have the determination she had,' Kannan responded.

'I am not like Kausalai, but what are you going to do with me?'

'That's what I don't know. I'm unable to move past you. I'm unable to let go of you. What do you think I should do?'

'You tell me.'

'I haven't thought about it.'

'I'll tell you. Will you listen to me?'

'How can I not listen to you? It feels like I'm living for you. You tell me, I'll listen. What should I do?'

'You should live well.'

'So be it!'

'I want to live with you!'

'Stay. Let your family come and kick us!'

'Why are they going to kick us? Listen to what I have to say.'

'Tell me.'

'As soon as Kausalai's matters are over, pay off your loans. If we get a reasonable price, let's sell the house. If not, we can deal with it later. Let's rent it to some good people and the two of us can travel to various places!'

'You are asking me to tag along with you, right?' Kannan asked.

'I am saying I will tag along with you!' Hema replied.

'Can you just go from place to place like that forever?'

'We will do that for a short period—just three months. You will also come to peace with yourself in that much time. After that, let's live in Kanchipuram. You can find work there,' Hema concluded.

'Let's see.'

'Say yes!'

'Do I have to say it? I can't do anything else.'

'Stop talking as if you've lost your confidence. You can achieve everything. I am asking you to save me.'

'Hmm...that's what I told you. The gutter will show us the way out!' Kannan said.

'That's the second time you have said that. I will convert the gutter into the Kaveri. I will behave that way. Wouldn't you be happy then?' Hema asked earnestly.

'You wouldn't fall into the water, would you?'

'No. I will not let go of you like that!'

'I thought everything was over, but something new is beginning!'

'Yes!'

'Is it raining?' Kannan asked.

'Yes, it was drizzling when I came here,' Hema answered.

'I think it's raining hard. Now, I am so afraid of the rain!'

'Even when I am here?'
Silence.
'Now I'm happy!'